THEY FOUGHT AT DEADMAN BUTTE

Larry Mangrum—He gave up the gunslick trade, but now it's calling him back—to certain death at the hands of a cold-blooded killer.

Molly Wells—Loyal to her outlaw father, she's falling in love with Mangrum. But her father is going to prison for twenty years, and Mangrum's headed for a showdown with the fastest gun in the West.

Pete Wells—He'd ridden the outlaw trail, then tried to go straight. Now he's going straight to prison—with his wife and daughter watching.

Jack Parris—A bounty hunter, he values money over life. There's a price on the head of Pete Wells, and Parris will get it—if he has to kill everyone riding on the Rawlins stage.

Marshal John Claxton—He's bringing the outlaw Wells in handcuffs to Rawlins. But in order to get there he has to trust Wells with his life.

Two Thumbs—The renegade Sioux chief likes to kill whites. But not right away. First he has his fun.

The Stagecoach Series
Ask your bookseller for the books you have missed

STATION 1: DODGE CITY
STATION 2: LAREDO
STATION 3: CHEYENNE
STATION 4: TOMBSTONE
STATION 5: VIRGINIA CITY
STATION 6: SANTA FE
STATION 7: SEATTLE
STATION 8: FORT YUMA
STATION 9: SONORA
STATION 10: ABILENE
STATION 11: DEADWOOD
STATION 12: TUCSON
STATION 13: CARSON CITY
STATION 14: CIMARRON
STATION 15: WICHITA
STATION 16: MOJAVE
STATION 17: DURANGO
STATION 18: CASA GRANDE
STATION 19: LAST CHANCE
STATION 20: LEADVILLE
STATION 21: FARGO
STATION 22: DEVIL'S CANYON
STATION 23: EL PASO
STATION 24: MESA VERDE
STATION 25: SAN ANTONIO
STATION 26: TULSA
STATION 27: PECOS
STATION 28: EL DORADO
STATION 29: PANHANDLE
STATION 30: RAWHIDE
STATION 31: ROYAL COACH
STATION 32: TAOS
STATION 33: DEATH VALLEY
STATION 34: DEADMAN BUTTE

STAGECOACH STATION 34:

DEADMAN BUTTE

Hank Mitchum

™

Created by the producers of
Wagons West, White Indian,
Badge, and Winning the West.

Book Creations Inc., Canaan, NY · Lyle Kenyon Engel, Founder

BANTAM BOOKS

TORONTO · NEW YORK · LONDON · SYDNEY · AUCKLAND

STAGECOACH STATION 34: DEADMAN BUTTE

A Bantam Book / published by arrangement with
Book Creations, Inc.

Bantam edition / March 1988

Produced by Book Creations, Inc.
Lyle Kenyon Engel: Founder

ISBN 0-553-27070-2

Published simultaneously in the United States and Canada

PRINTED IN THE UNITED STATES OF AMERICA

KR   0 9 8 7 6 5 4 3 2 1

STAGECOACH STATION 34:

DEADMAN BUTTE

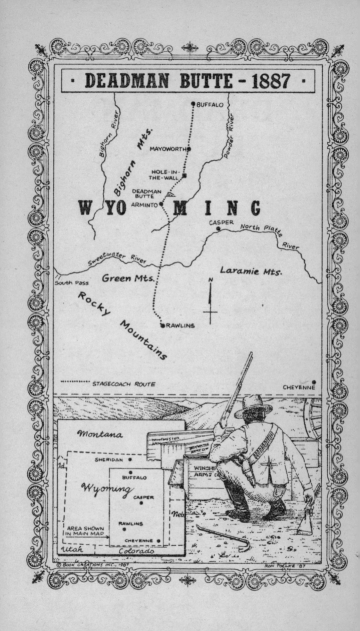

Chapter One

Yellow sunlight was spreading over the eastern horizon at the Bar S Ranch, seven miles west of Buffalo, Wyoming. Larry Mangrum and Gus Leonard, two of the twenty-odd ranch hands at the Bar S, saddled up and rode toward Buffalo, heading straight into the light of the rising sun. It was seven-thirty, and if they rode at a moderate pace they could be in town by eight o'clock.

As they rode away from the jumble of low-roofed buildings that made up the center of the ranch, following the wagon ruts that served as a road, twenty-two-year-old Larry Mangrum was quiet and pensive. A strikingly handsome young man, he had a square-cut jaw, prominent cheekbones, and coal-black, curly hair. Standing three inches over six feet before he slid into his boots, he was rangy but quite muscular, and he wore the mien of a man who knew what he was doing.

His friend, Gus Leonard, was four inches shorter, twenty pounds heavier, and two years older. After riding in silence for several minutes, Leonard spoke up, asking, "Hey, Larry, something bothering you?"

Adjusting his hat and shifting his position in the saddle, Larry Mangrum responded, "Last night Dennis Copeland told me about a telegram that's waiting for me in town. He

1

said that the Western Union operator had instructions to hand it to me personally, and that has me a little nervous. The only people who know I'm here are my parents and a few friends in Rawlins. I can't figure why any of them would send a telegram with instructions like that."

"Probably something private from your ma and pa. Family business, I mean. Maybe they don't want to take a chance on anyone else nosing in."

"Can't think of anything of that nature." The cowhand sighed. After pondering it for a moment, he said, "Gus, you don't suppose something has happened to one of them—my parents, I mean? Maybe someone in Rawlins is wiring me a death notice, or—"

"Hold on, pardner," cut in Leonard. "Now there's no sense in you borrowing trouble. Let's just wait till you can read the telegram. It's probably nothing of earth-shattering import." Attempting to divert his friend's bent for worry, he added, "I don't recall you ever telling me what your pa does for a living. In fact, in the six months you've been at the Bar S you haven't said much about home at all. Your pa a rancher?"

"No. He's a preacher."

Arching his eyebrows in slight surprise, Gus Leonard echoed, "A preacher?"

"Yep. He's pastor at the Rawlins Baptist Church."

Leonard was quiet for a moment and then commented, "So that's why you don't cuss or smoke or drink."

Larry Mangrum cleared his throat. "I'm, uh . . . not quite as pure as you've got it pictured, Gus. As for smoking, that just never appealed to me. But to be honest with you, I used to drink pretty heavily. I finally saw that it would get me nothing but trouble, so I quit. As for swearing, I've done my share. You just haven't seen me angry enough."

Gus Leonard nodded, giving his dark-haired friend a sidelong glance and a weak smile.

As the sun's heat began to blanket the land, a hot wind

from the west pelted the two riders with dirt and dust, and a large tumbleweed bounded in front of them as they rode into Buffalo. Leonard waved at an old-timer who sat on a bench along the boardwalk as they hauled up in front of the Western Union office.

As the two dusty men passed through the door, the Western Union operator smiled, revealing a set of poorly made dentures. Herman Otis was in his late sixties and thin as a rail. Looking over the half-moon spectacles that bridged his nose, he said, "Good mornin', boys. What can I do for you?"

"Howdy," Larry responded. "I think you've got a telegram for me. Larry Mangrum."

"That I do." The old man nodded. "In fact, I've got two of them. A second one came in not fifteen minutes ago." With that he pulled two sealed envelopes from a pigeon-hole behind the desk. Separating them, he said, "This is the one that came in yesterday, and this is the one that is still warm." Setting his narrow eyes on the lanky cowhand, he added, "You must be a pretty popular fella, son."

Larry Mangrum took the two envelopes and eyed them. The first one was dated July 17, 1889; the second, July 18, 1889.

As he was about to open the first one, the old man said, "I think that second one must be from a relative. Reverend Richard Mangrum?"

"Oh, sure," said Larry, apprehension in his voice. "That's my dad." Immediately he ripped open the second envelope, unfolded the telegram, and read it hurriedly, puzzlement clouding his face. Licking his lips nervously, he opened the other envelope and quickly read its message. His features lost color.

"What's wrong?" Gus Leonard asked.

Ignoring the question, Larry thanked Herman Otis and then stepped toward the door. Over his shoulder he said, "I'll tell you about it on the way home, Gus. Let's go."

Shaking his head, Gus Leonard followed.

Larry Mangrum was still at the door when he saw the dark figure standing at the edge of the boardwalk, outlined sharply by the brightness of the sunstruck street. Low on his right hip was a Colt .45, thonged to his slender thigh. Set in a homely, sober visage were a pair of steady eyes with a metallic cast to them. In a biting tone the man said, "Your name's Mangrum, ain't it?"

"Who's asking?" Larry snapped back, tight-lipped.

"Marty Fulton," came the quick reply, with a cocky wag of his head. "You've heard of me." It was a statement, not a question.

"Yeah." Larry nodded. "But you're wasting your time. As you can plainly see, I'm not wearing a gun."

Fulton spit on the boardwalk without taking his eyes off Larry. "Well, go get one. I'm itchin' to carve another notch in my gun."

Gus Leonard stepped up beside his friend and said to Fulton, "This sure sounds like gunhawk lingo to me, Fulton. Larry is a cowpoke, not a gunfighter."

Fulton's mouth curved into a wicked grin. "You must not know him very well, mister. Ask him about the big-timers he's put in their graves."

Leonard swung his eyes to Mangrum, who said to Fulton, "Go bark up another tree. I'm not wearing a gun, and I'm not putting one on."

Fulton whipped out his gun and thumbed back the hammer in one smooth move. "You'll brace me in a shootout, or you'll crawl the length of Main Street on your yellow belly!" he challenged.

A crowd was gathering, and Larry knew he was on the spot. He was going to have to take action. Looking around at the growing throng and then quickly setting his eyes on Fulton, he said, "Okay, Fulton. You'll get your gunfight. My gun's in my saddlebags, and you're standing between me and my horse."

A smile of triumph spread over Marty Fulton's face.

Relaxing slightly, he eased the hammer down on the revolver.

Larry Mangrum took a half step toward Fulton and then seized the gunfighter's hand with catlike speed, twisting the weapon from his grip. Fulton swore and howled with pain, swinging a fist at Larry's face.

Larry started to duck, but the blow glanced off his left ear. Tossing the gunfighter's revolver into a nearby water trough, he jammed an elbow into Fulton's rib cage, and the gunfighter grunted and doubled over in pain. Taking a step back, Mangrum growled, "Now it can stop right here, Fulton, or it can get a lot more rough. Choice is yours."

Gritting his teeth, Fulton straightened up. "Fists don't kill like bullets do," he said thinly. "You're scared to draw against me 'cause you know I'd kill you."

"You can think what you want," Larry rasped. "My beating you to a pulp will not change your mind. I'm tired of gunfights. I'm tired of the smell of burnt gunpowder, and I'm tired of leaving men dead in the street."

Fulton swore and spit, and then charged Larry with fists pumping like pistons. "We'll see who's gonna beat who to a pulp!" he roared.

Larry Mangrum chopped him behind the ear as he came in. The gunfighter went down but sprang back to his feet. He charged again, but this time he wrapped his arms around the taller man and rammed him into the hitch rail. The nearby horses nickered nervously, dancing about and pulling at the reins tied to the rail.

Somebody in the crowd said, "I'm goin' after the sheriff!"

Larry bounced off the hitch rail, twisted in the grasp of Fulton's arms, and put a headlock on him. The two of them hit the street hard, rolling and snorting. Within seconds they had broken from each other's grasp and were back on their feet. Once more they went at each other, again hitting the hitch rail, but this time sailing over it and landing with a hard jolt on the boardwalk.

Voices in the crowd began to cheer for Larry Mangrum

as they realized he was with Gus Leonard, whom they knew well. For his part, Leonard stood and watched the scuffle, half numbed. In the six months he had known Larry Mangrum, he had never suspected that Larry was a gunfighter.

Marty Fulton rolled from under Larry's weight and kicked him in the face. Larry bristled like a bulldog as he rolled free of a second kick. Standing up quickly, he looked hard at Fulton, who was also gaining his feet.

Larry ran the back of his hand across his face where Fulton's boot had struck him and found that the skin had broken. When he saw the blood, he breathed hotly, "Okay, Fulton. I told you it could get rough. I'm through playing with you now."

A wicked light danced in Marty Fulton's eyes. "Well, come on, cowboy. Let's get on with it." As he spoke, he came at Larry again, fists pumping.

The angry cowhand bobbed, weaved, and slammed a right to Fulton's jaw, whipping the man's head to the side. Just as he was bringing it back, Larry caught him with the other fist. The impact popped like an ax hitting a green tree, and Fulton's knees buckled. When Mangrum hit him square on the nose with another blow, Fulton went down, his nose spurting blood. He rolled toward the street and staggered to his feet, wagging his head. Then, releasing an animallike roar, he came at the taller man again.

Larry steadied himself and drove a powerful blow to the hollow of Fulton's jaw. Bone cracked, and the gunfighter left his feet from the impact. He was out cold when his back slammed onto the street.

At that moment Sheriff Glenn Watkins appeared. Standing over the crumpled form of Marty Fulton, Watkins looked at Larry and said, "You're one of the new cowhands from the Bar S, aren't you?"

"Yeah," Larry said, picking up his hat and brushing it off. He was covered with dust, and his face was streaked with blood from where Fulton had kicked him.

"What's this all about?"

Giving the sheriff his name, Larry told him the story in brief, and Gus Leonard and the clustered spectators backed him up. The sheriff, hoisting the unconscious man onto his shoulder, looked at Larry and said, "After the doc sees him, I'll let this troublemaker cool his heels in a cell for a few days. When he's ready to say he'll leave town, I'll turn him loose. But I'll warn him to stay away from you, Mangrum."

Gus Leonard grinned and said, "I doubt that'll be necessary, Sheriff. If the fella has any sense at all, he'll leave Larry alone."

Watkins agreed and then walked away bearing his burden. Gus Leonard turned and looked at Larry Mangrum, who observed the gravity on his friend's suntanned face. Leonard was about to speak when Larry said first, "Hey, Gus, don't look so serious. Yes, it's true; I used to be a gunfighter. But I gave it up."

Leonard's face muscles relaxed and he smiled. "Okay, pal," he said softly, "but I would like to hear about it. Why don't we go over to the Red Dog? It's still our day off, and I need a drink. You can tell me about it over there."

Larry agreed, and the two men made their way across the street amid congratulatory remarks from people of the town who had seen the fight. Mangrum smiled at them but made few comments.

The two men left the brilliant sunlight and entered the Red Dog Saloon and approached the bar. Gus Leonard ordered whiskey for himself and sarsaparilla for his teetotaler friend. By the time their drinks were ready, their eyes had adjusted to the comparative gloom of the place, and they carried their glasses to a corner table and sat down.

Leonard removed his hat, laid it on an empty chair, and fished his tobacco pouch from a shirt pocket. While he rolled a cigarette, he said, "Okay, pal, let's hear it."

Larry thumbed his hat to the back of his head, eased back in the chair, and said, "Gus, I've been less than honest with you and everyone at the Bar S. I never told the boss why I came to Buffalo. You sure you want to hear this?"

Leonard stuck the cigarette in the corner of his mouth and flared a match with his thumbnail. Touching the flame to the tip of the cigarette, he said, "I'm all ears."

As Gus Leonard listened intently, Larry Mangrum told his story. When he was nineteen, he had turned his back on the strict upbringing his parents had given him and began to run with a rowdy crowd, rebelling against the sheltered life he had lived. Soon after, he decided he wanted to live the glamorous, exciting life of a gunfighter. This aspiration broke his parents' hearts, and their grief grew deeper when their son took up drinking. He brought shame upon them, but they never disowned him or shut him out of their lives. Though they did not approve of the way he was living, they continued to show him that they loved him dearly.

Schooled by an aging gunfighter who had hung up his guns, young Larry Mangrum soon found that he had a natural ability with a sidearm, and he became fast and accurate with the .45 on his hip.

Taking another sip from his glass of sarsaparilla, Larry said, "By the time I turned twenty, I had challenged and killed four well-known gunfighters in southern Wyoming."

"Mind if I ask who they were?" Leonard asked, downing a shot of whiskey.

"First one was Billy Dearborn."

"Dearborn?" Leonard repeated. "I've heard of him. Knew he was cut down over in Rock Springs. Didn't know who did it."

"Second was Arlie Harris."

"Never heard of him," commented Leonard. "The third?"

"Apache Jim Wyman."

"Apache Jim? Really?"

"Yep."

"Happened at Laramie, didn't it?"

"Yeah. I got the fourth one in Laramie, too. Just three days after the shootout with Apache Jim. Name was Chet Stone."

Gus Leonard dropped his cigarette. "*Chet Stone?*" he gasped. "Say pal, you really were making a name for yourself, weren't you?"

"I guess you could say that."

"Well, then. Something must've happened to turn you away from pushing it further."

"Mm-hmm. About seven months ago I was home in Rawlins when a greenhorn named Duke Billings came into the saloon where I was drinking. We had heard of each other, and we both knew that the other was climbing the gunfighter's ladder. I was pretty drunk, and Duke got that way after a while. I'm not really sure just which one of us challenged the other, but even though I was drunk as a skunk, I got the draw on him and killed him."

"You don't remember it?" Leonard asked.

"Well, yeah," Larry replied, "but it's all pretty hazy. Of course, the haze cleared up real fast when Duke managed to put a bullet in my left shoulder before he died. And then it happened."

"What?"

"The thing that made me wise up and get out of the gunfighter business."

"I'm listening." Leonard leaned forward, eager to hear the rest.

"Less than five minutes after I killed Billings, the batwings swung open, and in walked a tall man with two holsters tied down. He was flanked by two cronies. After kneeling next to Duke's bloody corpse for a few minutes, he stood up and asked which one was Larry Mangrum. I was seated in a chair being attended to by the town's doctor. From where I sat, I told him I was Mangrum. He looked me in the eye and said, 'I understand you just killed Duke.' I assured him that I had. Then he said, 'I'm Vic Spain.' "

Gus Leonard sat up straight in his chair and gasped, "*Vic Spain?*"

"In person. And, Gus, the devil seemed to be looking at me right through his eyes when he said it."

"Larry, boy, Vic Spain is the fastest and most feared gunhawk west of the wide Missouri!"

"You're not telling me anything I don't know," came Larry's quick reply. "Spain told me that Duke Billings was his nephew, his sister's son. And then with a voice cold as an arctic wind he said he was going to kill me. But he wouldn't draw on me then because killing a drunk man who was bleeding with a gunshot wound would have put a blot on his reputation—and there was a big crowd in the saloon."

Leaning halfway across the table, Leonard said, "So what did he do?"

"Before he left, he pointed a stiff finger at me and said, 'I don't draw against wounded men who are full of whiskey, kid. But I'm makin' you a promise. I'll be back after your shoulder heals. Count on it. You killed my nephew, and you're gonna pay. You just be sober when I come back to Rawlins. You and me are gonna have us a shootout.' "

Gus Leonard gave a low whistle and then said, "If this is why you left Rawlins, I can't say that I blame you."

"That's why, all right." Larry pulled the two telegrams from his shirt pocket. "But now Spain is back in Rawlins looking for me."

"You mean one of those telegrams was from Spain?"

Looking grim, Larry handed his friend both envelopes, saying, "The top one is the one that came this morning. Read it first. It's from my parents."

Leonard held Larry's gaze briefly as he took the envelopes, and then he pulled out the top one and read it aloud: " 'Do not come home, son. Spain will not hurt us.

We do not care what people here say about you. We want you alive. We love you. Mother and Dad.' "

His sun-darkened features showing concern, Leonard laid the telegram on the table and proceeded to read the other one aloud: " 'I am back in Rawlins to brace you. They tell me you are not yellow. We will see. If you care about people here, come to the Wyoming Hotel. Be sober this time. Vic Spain.' " Leonard's face pinched as he said, "Larry, you can't go back there and draw against Spain! It'd be suicide!"

Larry took a deep breath and let it out slowly. "I have to, Gus. Spain is threatening to do harm to my parents. You read what they said, trying to convince me that he won't hurt them. He may have more than just my parents in mind, too. I can't let that dirty snake in the grass harm *anybody* because of me."

"But, Larry," argued Leonard, "it isn't gonna help you or your parents if you get killed. You saw what your parents said. They don't want you to face Spain."

Shaking his head, Mangrum said somberly, "I couldn't live with myself if my parents or anyone else got hurt because I was too cowardly to face Spain. I've already brought plenty of shame on the Mangrum name. I can't add cowardice to it, too."

"Yeah, but being killed is no way—"

Throwing palms up, Larry cut in, "I appreciate your concern, Gus, but the die is cast! I have no choice. Like it or not, I have to face Vic Spain." Pushing his chair away from the table, the dark-haired young man rose. Looking at Leonard, he said, "I'm going to the stage office right now and book a seat on the next stage to Rawlins."

Knowing further words would be of no avail, Gus Leonard followed his friend to the Buffalo Stage Line office, where they learned that the stage to Rawlins ran twice a week and that it would be leaving the next day. Larry bought a ticket, and then he and Leonard headed toward the ranch.

While the hot wind buffeted his face, Larry Mangrum rode in silence, a cold dread washing over him. Gus Leonard was right; facing Spain would be suicide. But he clearly had no choice.

It had to be done.

Chapter Two

Thirty minutes after the two Bar S cowhands had left Buffalo, U.S. Marshal John Claxton rode into town, facing into a blustering July wind that felt like a blast from a furnace. A swirling dust devil whipped sand into the lawman's face as several tumbleweeds rolled across his path, disappearing within seconds between weather-faded buildings.

Reining in at the Johnson County sheriff's office, the broad-shouldered, heavyset man in his midfifties eased stiffly from the saddle and wrapped the reins around the hitch rail. He paused long enough to stretch his six-foot frame and to remove his hat, mopping the sweat from his bald pate. Though the top of his head lacked hair, he wore a heavy, drooping mustache that was salted with gray, as were his temples and sideburns. Dropping the hat in place, he pulled the gun belt up tight against his ample belly and entered the hot, stuffy office.

Sheriff Glenn Watkins looked up from behind the desk as Claxton's hulking frame filled the doorway. Watkins stood up, a smile spreading across his face as he rounded the desk, extending his hand. "Well, I'll be a monkey's uncle, if it isn't John Claxton!"

As the two lawmen clasped hands, Watkins said, "How long has it been, John? Four years?"

"Something like that, Glenn." Claxton grinned. "I think it was when I passed through here while taking a couple of outlaws to Rawlins—that was in, uh . . . April of eighty-five. Yep, it's been more than four years."

Gesturing for the marshal to sit down in a chair in front of the desk, Watkins, who was about fifty and had graying sandy hair, returned to his own. Opening a small wooden humidor, he produced two cigars and handed one to Claxton. As they were lighting the cigars, Watkins asked, "Where are you headed now, John?"

"Right here," replied the potbellied man. "I got an anonymous tip a few days ago while I was over at Sundance. I came out of a café and found a note stuck to my saddle that said Pete Wells was living in Buffalo."

Sheriff Glenn Watkins settled back in his chair, blew smoke toward the ceiling, and said, "Somebody's sent you on a wild goose chase, John. I know everybody who lives in or near this town. There's no Pete Wells living here. What's he wanted for?"

"Stagecoach robbery, mainly, but he did hit a couple of banks down in Colorado about three years ago. I've been on his trail for over five years. It's been well over two since I lost all track of him. I thought maybe he fell in a crack somewhere and died. There've been no reports of him pulling any jobs since that time."

"Well, he must be buried in that crack," chuckled Watkins. "Like I said, there's no Pete Wells living in or around Buffalo."

"Let me ask you this," said Claxton, leaning forward. "Have you got a family living around here that goes by the name of Sheridan?"

"Yep." The sheriff nodded. "Man's name is Fred. Works for J. D. Ryle over at the blacksmith shop."

"Tell me about him," Claxton said.

"Well, he's about forty. Wife's name is Betty. They have a nineteen-year-old daughter, Molly—honey-blond hair like her mother and prettier than a rose petal." Suddenly his brow furrowed. "You're not about to tell me that Fred Sheridan is Pete Wells?"

Claxton knocked ashes from the cigar, letting them float to the floor. Leaning forward in his chair, he said, "Fred Sheridan is about forty, you say?"

"Yeah."

"Stands about five-ten, has pale blue eyes, sandy hair, and weighs about a hundred and ninety?"

Glenn Watkins paused before answering. The marshal's news was disturbing. His voice tightening, he replied, "Yeah."

Claxton's next words came almost in a monotone. "Pete Wells is exactly forty years of age. His wife, Betty, is thirty-nine and has honey-blond hair. Their daughter, Molly, is the image of her mother, and when I started chasing her father five years ago, Molly was fourteen years old. Pete Wells has sandy hair, stands five-ten, weighs a hundred and ninety, and has pale blue eyes."

Claxton saw the words shatter the sheriff's composure. Watkins whispered a curse, banging his fist on the desk. Shaking his head in disbelief, he choked, "I can't believe it, John. I just . . . can't believe it. Fred Sheridan and his family have lived in Buffalo for two years, and everybody loves them. They're active in the Methodist church—Fred even serves on the board of deacons—and Betty and Molly are very popular with the women in town. J. D. Ryle says Fred is the best man he has ever had working for him! Something's just not right here. There must be some mistake."

At that point, Claxton reached in his shirt pocket and produced two neatly folded pieces of paper. Unfolding them both, he laid them on the desk in front of the frustrated sheriff, smoothing them with his hands. One was a wanted poster, bearing a photograph of outlaw Pete Wells and offering a five-thousand-dollar reward for his capture; the second was a warrant for Pete Wells's arrest. As the sheriff's eyes fixed on the face on the poster,

Claxton said, "Now tell me there's a mistake. Is that your Fred Sheridan?"

Watkins, his gray eyes sorrowful, slowly met the marshal's gaze. Swallowing hard, he nodded silently.

"Seems like Wells has wrapped this town around his little finger, Glenn," said Claxton. "Including you. Apparently he has been a model citizen. But that doesn't change the fact that the man is an outlaw. He's wanted, and I've got to arrest him and take him to Rawlins for trial."

Standing up, Watkins laid his cigar in a glass ashtray, sighed, and said, "It's too bad. Fred Sheridan has been a blessing to this town. We were about to elect him to the town council!" He shook his head. "I've been a lawman for twenty-two years, John, and I thought I could spot a criminal a mile off, but he sure fooled me. Such a nice guy . . . always there to help anybody who needed it, and never asking for anything in return. It's hard to picture him robbing banks and stagecoaches."

"Some of them are slick," commented Claxton, also rising. "I'm going to need you to get me a few men to aid in arresting him. I suppose he's at the blacksmith shop right now."

"Most likely he is," the sheriff solemnly confirmed. "But I don't think you'll need an army, John. If I go with you, he'll give up without a fight. I'm sure of it."

Claxton eyed the sheriff with doubtful speculation. "I don't think you know who we're dealing with here, Glenn. Wells is an outlaw and a robber. He's a dangerous man."

"Has he ever killed anybody?"

"No, but he pulled a gun on a lot of people."

"I still say he can be arrested without a fight if I go with you."

Shrugging his bulky shoulders, Claxton said, "Okay, my friend. I'll take your word for it. Let's go."

*   *   *

The sun was climbing higher as a lone rider hauled up in front of an old unpainted shack on the north edge of Buffalo. The wind plucked at the long hair dangling in matted strands beneath the man's sweat-stained hat. Sliding from the saddle, he adjusted the gun belt on his hips and stepped onto the creaky porch, banging on the door with his fist. Inside there was instant movement, the sound of footsteps, and then the door opened, the rusty hinges squealing their complaint.

An unkempt old man appeared, with watery eyes, tousled gray hair, and the smell of an unbathed body. Above his grimy trousers he wore only his long johns, which were gray from extended use without laundering. In his hand was a nearly empty bottle of whiskey. When his bleary eyes focused on the hatchet-faced visitor with the blue stubble on his cheeks, the oldster exposed his toothless gums in a wide smile and said, "Howdy, Jack. I been lookin' for you. Come on in."

The hinges squealed again as Willie Hooks opened the door wider to allow his friend, Jack Parris, to pass through. Parris did not smell so good himself, but even so the stench of the shack's interior came as a shock. The trapped heat enhanced the stench, and as the old man started to close the door, Parris said, "Leave it open, Willie. It's like an oven in here."

Shrugging his thin shoulders, Willie Hooks let go of the door and pointed with the dirty whiskey bottle to a rickety chair. "Set a spell, Jack. This bottle's about empty, and it's my last, but how about some coffee? It was fresh this mornin'."

Parris did not trust the chair to hold his weight. Stepping to the soot-covered stove, he looked into the coffeepot, the sight of the sludge in the bottom turning his stomach. "No thanks," he said. "I'm not in the mood for coffee, and I'll stand if you don't mind."

"Well, suit yourself," cackled the old man, lifting the bottle and downing the rest of its contents. Belching loudly, he threw the bottle in a corner. His fingers raked at his patchy beard and then scratched under both arms. "Sure didn't take you long to get here."

Setting his calculating eyes on the oldster, Parris grunted. "Willie, this good news of yours better be plenty good. It's been a long, hot ride from Bozeman."

Willie's mouth split into a joyful grin. The deep lines and craggy wrinkles on his leathered face were a telltale calendar of his advancing years. Squinting at the younger man, he said, "Is a fast four thousand dollars good news?"

"Four thousand!" exclaimed Parris.

"It's actually five thousand," Willie said, "but the information will cost you a thousand. I figure four thousand oughta satisfy a thirty-five-year-old bounty hunter like yourself. I can rightly say a thousand will satisfy an old coot like me."

"I'm thirty-two," Parris replied blandly. With dollar signs almost visible in his eyes, he said, "Now tell me about this five thousand."

Willie crossed the small room, poured himself a cup of the lukewarm, syrupy black coffee, and said, "You know how I make my livin'."

"Yeah. Scrounging around town, poking into people's trash so you can find something to salvage and sell for a few dollars."

"Well, you don't have to say it in that tone of voice," the old man said defensively. "It's honest work."

"Can't deny that," admitted Parris.

Willie scratched his ribs. "At least I don't make my way in life gunnin' down outlaws for pay."

Parris brushed his nose with a knuckle. "Society offers the reward, and I risk my neck to collect it. Now let's get on with it."

"Well, it's like this," said Willie. "A few days ago—the same day I sent you the wire—I was siftin' through the trash of a relatively new family in town. Folks named Sheridan. They've lived here about two years. The man's called Fred, and his wife's Betty. Daughter's Molly. Purty as a picture. She has long, sunny-colored hair and—"

"Willie, I'm not interested in all that. Just tell me what you're getting at."

The old man smiled again and said, "Sorry. Anyway, in these people's trash I found some papers that I'm sure were supposed to be burned but must've been blowed from the ash pit. I'd have overlooked 'em myself except that one had Fred Sheridan's picture on it! It was one of them wanted-dead-or-alive posters—only the poster said his name is Pete Wells."

Parris's eyes widened. "Pete Wells! I've heard of him. Bank and stagecoach robber. He's wanted in Colorado and Wyoming."

Shuffling across the room to a littered cupboard, Willie picked up some papers and returned to his friend. "Here it is," he said. "Right on top."

Jack Parris took the partially burned poster and examined it closely. "Sure enough! Five thousand dollars reward." Giving Willie a hard look, he said, "You're dead sure the face on this poster is this Fred Sheridan?"

"No doubt about it," responded the old man. "And looky here," he said, extending the other papers to Parris. "Here's four letters addressed to Peter Wells in Denver, Colorado. They're dated three and four years ago. At least that's the way it is on three of 'em. One is burned too bad to tell."

Parris looked the letters over, his thin face alive with avarice. "Sure enough, Willie. This guy posing as Fred Sheridan is Pete Wells, all right." A wicked light danced in his eyes. "You've got a deal, Willie. You'll get your thousand after I collect the money for bringing in Wells. Next thing I've got to do is figure out the best way to take him. Where does he live?"

"On Maple, two blocks east of Main Street," answered Willie. "But if you're lookin' to find him in the daytime, you'll find him at Ryle's Blacksmith Shop. That's where he works." Checking the angle of the sun through a dirty fly-specked window, he added, "Probably be at the shop until lunch, for another hour or so."

"How many work there?"

"Just him and J. D. Ryle, the owner."

Parris pondered the situation for a long moment, and then rubbing his bristled chin, he mumbled, "Yeah. That's how I'll do it."

"What's that?" Willie Hooks asked.

Setting his eyes on the wrinkled face of the old man, the bounty hunter said, "I was just deciding how I'll take him. I'll tie my horse right near the door of the shop, see, and when I go inside, I'll ask for Sheridan, tell him my horse has something wrong with a shoe, and ask him to come out and look at it. When I get him bent over looking at the shoe, I'll put my gun on him!"

Willie scratched under his left arm. "But what if J. D. decides he should be the one to look at the shoe?"

"I'll insist on Sheridan. I'll say that a friend of mine who used to live in Buffalo recommended him to me. He liked the work that Sheridan did and told me not to let anyone else do it. Yeah, that'll take care of it."

"Should," agreed the old man.

Eager to get on with his deed, Jack Parris folded the wanted poster and stuck it in the pocket of his sweaty shirt. Heading for the door, he said, "I'll see you later, pal."

The instant Parris stepped out into the hot wind, he noticed how good it smelled. Willie's squalid shack stunk worse than any pigsty or barnyard the bounty hunter had ever seen. As he mounted his horse, he watched as the old man came onto the porch and, scratching, said, "Ain'tcha glad ol' Willie's got sharp eyes, Jack? You're gonna be rich, and I'm gonna be well off!"

Parris's long, greasy hair danced in the wind, and his beady eyes gleamed. "Yes, sir, eagle eye. You've done us both a favor. See you later."

* * *

Sheriff Glenn Watkins dropped his hat on his head and stepped past the marshal through the door of his office. Claxton followed, and the two lawmen walked together down the dusty street toward the blacksmith shop. Watkins greeted several people along the street, their faces filling with curiosity when they noted the U.S. marshal's badge on the chest of the big man who accompanied him.

The blacksmith shop was a log building with two huge chimneys protruding through the roof, smoke billowing from them both. Two large doors were propped open to allow ventilation. As the two men drew near, Watkins said, "John, why don't you let me do the talking? Let me approach him, okay?"

"Sure," agreed Claxton. "But I'll be ready to clobber him or shoot him if he puts up a struggle."

"I tell you it won't happen," said Watkins assuredly.

Watkins put himself two or three steps ahead of the federal man as they left the street and passed through the big open doors. Shifting his gaze quickly, the sheriff saw the man he knew as Fred Sheridan bent over, straddling a horse's hind leg, which he held up so that he could nail on a new horseshoe. Sheridan—Pete Wells—was just driving in the last nail.

J. D. Ryle was at an anvil about to pound a red-hot horseshoe into shape when he spotted the local lawman. The short, heavy man smiled and said, "Howdy, Glenn. Who's your friend?"

At that moment, Pete Wells looked up. He saw Watkins and a smile started to break on his lips, but it died when he saw the badge on the federal marshal's chest. Dropping the horse's leg, he straightened up, clenching the hammer so tightly in his hand that his knuckles turned white. His entire body went rigid.

Stepping close to him, the sheriff said in a calm tone,

"Fred, I have just been told by U.S. Marshal John Claxton here that you are Pete Wells, a wanted outlaw. Is this so?"

Looking over Watkins's shoulder, Claxton saw the fire ignite in Pete Wells's eyes as a mottled flush surfaced on his face. Claxton tensed, lowering his hand near the butt of his revolver. It appeared that Wells was going to fight.

Watkins, seeing the same thing, stepped closer and looked deep into the outlaw's eyes. Holding his voice steady, he said, "You've already answered my question. Now, please don't try to fight your way out of this. I will have to help the marshal arrest you, but I'm still your friend, Fred. Don't make me fight you."

Pete Wells gave a deep sigh, let the hammer slip through his hands, and said, "I knew this day had to come. Guess a man can't run away from the law forever."

John Claxton did not pull his gun. Moving closer, he said, "Pete Wells, I'm arresting you on twenty-seven counts of robbery. I will take you to Rawlins, where you will stand trial. You and I both know that the jury will convict you."

By this time, J. D. Ryle had drawn near. Amazement framed his sweaty face. He looked at Wells with sadness in his eyes and then said to Claxton, "Marshal, I don't doubt you know what you're doin', and Fred hasn't denied that he is the outlaw you're after, but doesn't the good a man does ever help to offset the bad?"

"Not with the law, sir," Claxton replied. "The man broke the law. He has to pay."

Pete Wells laid his hand on Ryle's shoulder. "J. D., you've been mighty good to me. I'll never forget you." The blacksmith's brow furrowed, and his eyes misted as Wells turned to the sheriff and said, "Glenn, somebody will have to watch out for Betty and Molly."

Ryle spoke up quickly, "If it's money you're talkin' about, Fred, I'll do my part to see that they have enough. I'm sure the rest of this town will pitch in, too."

His lips pulled tight, Wells thanked Ryle and then

turned to Claxton to ask, "How soon will we be going, Marshal?"

"Whenever the next stage is going to Rawlins," came the reply.

"That'll be tomorrow," said Watkins.

"Then tomorrow it'll be," confirmed Claxton.

"I have to lock you up now, Fred," said Watkins. "The marshal and I will go to your house and tell your family what has happened."

"You'll let them come and see me before we leave, won't you, Marshal?" asked the outlaw.

"Sure," said Claxton. "As long as they're looking at you through bars, I don't care how much they see you. I'll let the sheriff control that."

When Wells anxiously swung his gaze to Watkins, the sheriff said quickly, "As far as I'm concerned, Betty and Molly can camp outside your cell until the stage leaves tomorrow."

Solemnly nodding his sandy head, Wells said, "Thank you, Glenn. I appreciate it." Looking back at Claxton, he asked, "Marshal, would you mind telling me how you found me?"

Claxton thumbed his hat to the back of his bald head. "It was an anonymous tip. Somebody stuck a note to my saddle when I was over in Sundance, told me you were in Buffalo. I figure whoever it was didn't know of the five thousand dollar reward on your head, or he would have come forward so he could collect it. Probably somebody who's got it in for you about something."

"That's likely enough," Pete Wells said soberly. "When you run with the crowd I ran with, you come up against some tough birds. Serves me right. A man reaps what he sows."

Twenty minutes later the two lawmen left their prisoner in the jail and walked down the street to the office of the Buffalo Stage Line. Entering the office with John Claxton on his heels, Sheriff Glenn Watkins greeted the two men who were bent over a desk behind the counter. "Good morning," Watkins said as they looked up. "Ross Blake, Bill Owens, I want you to meet U.S. Marshal John Claxton."

Blake and Owens moved to the counter and reached over it to shake hands with Claxton as Watkins explained to the marshal that Ross Blake owned the company, with Bill Owens serving as general manager of the home office. Blake was a brown-haired, muscular man in his early forties with an angular face and brown eyes that spoke of dogged determination. He was handsome in a rugged sort of way. There was no doubt that the six-foot-four-inch owner of the Buffalo Stage Line was an assertive and aggressive man.

Bill Owens, by contrast, was a rather nondescript man in his midfifties. He was of medium height and build, and he carried a warm, friendly smile.

"What can we do for you gentlemen?" asked Blake.

"I need to book two seats on your stage to Rawlins tomorrow," Claxton explained. "One for me, and one for a prisoner I'm taking to Rawlins to stand trial. His name is Pete Wells. You know him as Fred Sheridan."

Shock registered on the faces of both men. Claxton went on to explain Wells's criminal record to the two astonished men, and when he had finished, Ross Blake commented that the whole town was going to be stunned. He then asked what was going to happen to Betty and Molly. Watkins told him of J. D. Ryle's offer of financial assistance, adding that he felt the people of Buffalo would see to it that the two women were taken care of. Both Blake and Owens said they would do their part.

Still shocked at the news, Blake said to Claxton, "The stage is due to arrive in here just before noon tomorrow, Marshal. It'll turn right around and head back."

As Claxton purchased the two tickets, he was told that at this point only one other passenger was booked for the trip, a cowboy from the Bar S Ranch named Mangrum.

Turning to Owens, the stage-line owner said, "Bill, will you check out that shipment going to Arminto?"

Being forward and friendly, Claxton adjusted the gun belt under his paunch and said, "How long have you been in the stagecoach business, Blake?"

As his assistant left the room, the rugged-looking stageowner said, "Exactly four years."

Claxton grinned and replied, "I'll bet I can tell you what you did before that."

Blake returned the grin, waiting for Claxton to speculate.

"You were in the army," the big marshal said flatly.

Blake raised his bushy eyebrows and smiled. "You're right."

His grin broadening, Claxton said, "And you were an officer. At least a captain."

Looking at the sheriff, Blake said, "Your friend, here, is some kind of a seer, Glenn." Swinging his gaze back to Claxton, he chuckled, "I was a captain. I didn't know it still showed."

"On you it'll show when you're a hundred," mused Claxton. "Where'd you serve?"

"Dakota Territory, Nebraska, Colorado, Wyoming, Montana. I was with Custer, Crook, and Fetterman in the bloody Indian campaigns. I married a beautiful woman back in seventy-nine, and I got tired of being away from her so much of the time that I mustered out in eighty-five. Decided I wanted to live a normal life. We settled here in Buffalo, and I started the line immediately after retiring from the army."

Claxton said cordially, "I'd like to meet your wife sometime, Mr. Blake."

Ross Blake's face stiffened. "That won't be possible, Marshal. Jenny died three years ago."

"Oh . . . I'm so sorry." Claxton's face tinted. "Please forgive me. I—"

"It's all right, Marshal," responded Blake. "How could you know? Jenny caught pneumonia just a year after we moved here. It took her almost overnight. I . . . I still miss her very much. All I have now is the business, so I've plunged in lock, stock, and barrel. By staying busy, I don't have as much time to be lonely for Jenny."

"Best thing to do," commented Claxton. Roving his gaze over the well-furnished office, he said, "Looks like you must be doing all right."

"The business has grown steadily." Blake smiled. "I'm running four coaches—two of them from Buffalo all the way north to Great Falls, and the other two from Buffalo south to Rawlins."

"Line hauls a lot of cargo, as well as people," put in Glenn Watkins.

As Bill Owens came in quietly and sat down at the desk, Blake turned to him. "Rifles and ammunition count out all right, Bill?"

"Yes." Owens nodded. "Two dozen Remington forty-fours and eight hundred rounds."

"Somebody starting a war?" queried the marshal.

"Not exactly," replied Blake. "Folks down in Arminto are having some trouble with renegade Sioux. A gun dealer in Billings is shipping the rifles to them so they can better protect themselves. The guns will be going on the stage tomorrow."

"It isn't Two Thumbs, is it?" asked Claxton.

"I don't think so," said Blake. "Two Thumbs seems to have been doing his dirty work in southeastern Montana for some time. I'm sure it's one of the other bands."

"They can be thankful for that. Two Thumbs is meaner than a snake with a sore belly. There isn't an ounce of mercy in him. You had any attacks on your stagecoaches by the Sioux?"

"Not as yet. We're keeping our fingers crossed. Of course, we have a little help, too."

"What do you mean?"

"Back in April, when the renegades started showing up all over southern Wyoming, Colonel Adams at Fort

Fetterman began sending regular patrols of over forty men each between the Deadman Butte area all the way down to Rawlins. Because stagecoaches are so vulnerable to Indian attack, Adams has been giving our coaches cavalry escorts from our way station at Deadman Butte clear into Rawlins. We feel relatively safe with these escorts."

"Yes, I should say so!" Claxton said.

Blake nodded, adding, "I just hope Two Thumbs stays in Montana. Who knows what he'd do if he should move into our territory? He's mean enough to try about anything. He might even pull enough Sioux warriors together to take on one of the cavalry escorts!"

Bill Owens looked up from his place at the desk and asked, "Any of you know why this Two Thumbs is so vicious?"

"Because he's Sioux," volunteered Watkins with a touch of bitterness in his voice.

"There's more to it than that!" Claxton boomed. "Two Thumbs is said to be a distant cousin of Crazy Horse—and we all know how much Crazy Horse hated whites. If I have it straight, it was Two Thumbs who first stirred up the Sioux to jump the reservations. He collected several bands of dissident warriors and turned them into renegades. Now they're running all over this part of the country killing whites."

"And that's not all," Ross Blake added. "Don't you fellas know how Two Thumbs got his name?"

Shrugging his thick shoulders, John Claxton said, "I figured it was just another of those silly Indian names. You know . . . when they're babies, they do something that sets them apart, and from that they are given their names. Seems I heard that he sucked both thumbs instead of only one like most babies, so his ma named him Two Thumbs."

"Sorry to contradict you, Marshal, but that's not it at all," said Blake, shaking his head. "That Indian's savage hatred for whites stems from what happened to his hands."

"Guess I hadn't heard that," said Claxton, lifting his hat

and scratching his bald head with the same hand. He obviously was unaccustomed to being corrected. "What happened?"

The former captain bent his tall frame, leaned his elbows on the counter, and said, "His name used to be Angry Wolf. Came simply from his vile nature and hot temper. Angry Wolf developed into one of the Hunkpapa Sioux's greatest warriors. He was a killer with any weapon he could get hold of, but he was best known for his prowess in hand-to-hand combat. He could take on three or four men at one time and kill them all, using only a knife or tomahawk. He fought with Crazy Horse, and stories are told that he killed dozens of white soldiers in hand-to-hand fighting. They say he was strong as a gorilla and fast as a cougar."

"You ever see him?" asked Glenn Watkins.

"Three times," came the quick reply. "Twice in the dust and smoke of battle, and once from a distance as he sat his big black horse. The third time was after he had been maimed."

Eager to hear more, Bill Owens said, "Well, come on, Ross. Tell us about it."

"Back in seventy-seven, about a year after the Custer massacre, a squad of cavalry troopers caught Angry Wolf and a handful of his best warriors in a box canyon in the Montana Rockies. By this time, Angry Wolf had been made a chief among the Hunkpapas. The troopers well outnumbered the Indians and quickly killed all but Angry Wolf. They left him alive on purpose—so that they could send a message to other Indians who might consider becoming renegades. The lieutenant in charge, Erick Simpson, had his men tie the Indian securely. Then, rather than kill him, Simpson maimed him so he could never fight effectively in hand-to-hand combat again. He cut off both of Angry Wolf's thumbs."

"Ah, I get it," spoke up Owens. "He did that so the

Indian could never properly wield a knife or a tomahawk again."

"Exactly." Blake nodded. "From that time on, both whites and Indians called him Two Thumbs. The shame he felt for what had happened to him was outweighed by his hatred for white men, especially for the lieutenant and the men who maimed him. In less than three months after the incident, Two Thumbs had trailed the whole squad and captured them. He had his warriors torture and kill every one of them. The last to die was Simpson. The warriors took him to a remote spot somewhere near Cheyenne, and under Two Thumbs's direction they chopped off all his fingers and toes, cut out his tongue, sliced off his ears, and then hung him to a tree limb by his ankles. They scalped him and let him hang there until he bled to death."

Bill Owens's face was chalky white.

"Now I know why Two Thumbs is so malicious," Claxton said to Blake. "I've heard some of the things he and his renegades have done to white people—the same kind of stuff you just told us about."

"There's a whole lot of it going on in southeastern Montana," said Blake. "Two Thumbs has concentrated on that area for over six months now. He's been wiping out wagon trains and settlers, always torturing them before killing them. The worst part is what he does to white women."

"I've heard some of it before," said Claxton. "I've been told that many of the settlers have seen Two Thumbs coming and killed their wives and daughters before the savage and his men could get to them."

"You're right." Blake nodded. "A report came in just two days ago that it happened exactly like that a few miles east of the Little Bighorn last month. The army found the remains of a wagon train—said what they saw was beyond belief. Especially what was done to the women, even after they were dead."

"So it's other Sioux bands that are bothering the people in Arminto, you say?" Claxton asked.

"Why haven't they wiped out the town?" said Owens. "It's not very big."

"Their bands are scattered, and they're small, most with about a dozen warriors each," said Blake. "At least that's what the army tells me. But things will get bad if the bands get together."

Claxton rubbed his chin. "Well, it's comforting to know that the stage my prisoner and I will be traveling on will have an army escort from Deadman Butte to Rawlins. I assume the reason they meet you there is because there has been no hostile activity farther north."

"That's right," confirmed Blake.

"I hope that doesn't change," the marshal grumbled. Turning to the sheriff, he said, "Well, Watkins, I guess we'd better go deliver the bitter message to Mrs. Wells and her daughter."

"Yeah," replied Watkins with a shaky sigh. Struggling against the sick feeling that was rising in his stomach, he said, "I'd rather take a beating with a horsewhip than have to break this awful news to those two women."

Pete Wells sat on the cot in his stuffy cell, staring blankly at the floor. His throat was dry, and a numb weariness had claimed him. He mentally lashed himself as he had already done a thousand times before. Why had he been so dumb as to take up a life of crime?

Wells figured his prison term would probably be at least twenty years. Maybe with good behavior he would be paroled in ten or eleven, but what would become of his family? The townspeople might help them for a while, but not indefinitely.

Burying his face in his hands, he pictured the moment Marshal Claxton would appear at the house to tell Betty and Molly that he had been arrested. Grinding his teeth, he silently wept.

Suddenly he heard a sound outside the cell window. Raising his head, he stood up, and at that instant a familiar voice called, "Hey, Fred! Can you hear me?" It was J. D. Ryle.

The cell window was near the ceiling, about seven feet high, so Wells moved a small stool beneath the window and stepped up. To his surprise, the alley behind the jail was jammed with people. They greeted him with smiles and called his name as his sandy-haired face appeared at the barred window. In the forefront were the blacksmith and Reverend Wallace Perkins, minister of the Methodist church. Ryle said, "Fred, the whole town knows about your arrest. I told them what the marshal said about you being an outlaw, and that you didn't deny it. But we would all like to hear what you have to say about it."

The elderly Reverend Perkins spoke up and said, "Son, we want you to know that we love you, no matter what you've done. We don't know what you were in the past, but we know what you are now. We're your friends, and we will stick by you."

As a chorus of voices punctuated the minister's words with agreement, Pete Wells blinked against the moisture that had surfaced in his eyes. His throat constricted with emotion.

"If it wouldn't be asking too much, son," said Perkins, "could you tell us a little about your past? We would rather hear it from you so no false stories can get started. After all, Betty and Molly are going to be here with us while you are gone, and we don't want them to have to live with false accusations about you."

"I appreciate that, Pastor," Pete Wells said past the lump in his throat. "But before I tell you the story, let me say that I'm not making any excuses for myself. I was wrong to become an outlaw. Please keep in mind that I am ashamed of what I did."

The crowd in the alley listened intently as Wells began his story. "I had a dryland farm in northeastern Colorado where I raised beef cattle and wheat. The drought in eighteen eighty-three wiped me out, and I had to do something to provide for my family. . . ."

Times had been hard. His small farm in eastern Colorado had turned to dust, and his cattle had died for lack of grass and water. He had tried hard to find a job but to no avail. Maybe he would have been able to find a way to provide for his family as other men did if it had not been for his son's illness. Bobby was so close to death, and Pete had to find a way to get the boy into the hospital at Denver. But they would not admit Bobby—no matter how sick he was—unless Pete could lay down at least a hundred dollars in cash.

Pete had no choice; his young son's life was at stake. Without telling Betty, he waylaid a stagecoach near Greeley, Colorado, robbing its passengers of over five hundred dollars. Bobby was admitted to the hospital, but it was too late. He died the very day he was admitted.

Pete thought of the awful moment when he had had to tell Betty how he had obtained the money. On top of losing her nine-year-old son to a lung disease, she had to learn that she was married to an outlaw. She had begged him to turn himself in to the Denver County sheriff, but he was sure he would go to prison. He refused, saying if he lay low for a while, the law would never catch him. He had worn a mask in the holdup and had ridden a stolen horse so he could not be identified.

Betty then begged him to send the money they had not spent on Bobby to the stage office, so that the passengers could at least get some of their money back. Wells had argued that they had no money, and it was more important that she and Molly have food and shelter. The passengers would survive.

Wells had earnestly continued to look for work, but he found nothing but short-term jobs that played out within a few days. By then they were living in a drafty hovel outside of Denver, and winter was coming. There was only one thing to do: He robbed more stagecoaches and put his wife and daughter in a nice house in Denver. Betty had quit trying to reason with him; she had Molly to think of. Wells continued his robbing spree, even hitting a few banks.

With the law on his heels, Wells could seldom go home, but he did have to show up periodically to give money to Betty. On one occasion when he had sneaked into town under cover of darkness to see his wife and daughter, Betty told him that a U.S. marshal named Claxton had been there looking for him.

Pete had eluded the law for the next three years while he continued his life of crime. Each time he saw Betty, she begged him to give it up, saying that Claxton was knocking on the door every few weeks. Finally, he told her they would move far away from Denver and he would find a job. They had enough money at last to make things work. When they landed in Buffalo, Wyoming, Wells was hired almost immediately by J. D. Ryle to work in the blacksmith shop.

Things had run smoothly for the past two years. Living under the name of Sheridan, Pete, Betty, and Molly had been incredibly happy, he told the group gathered outside the jail.

And now their world was crashing down upon them.

Chapter Three

The hot summer sun was punishing the land already. Betty and Molly Wells built a fire under a large galvanized tub of hot water in the shade of two cottonwood trees behind their house. As the water heated, the gusty wind continually swirled smoke around the tub and then carried it away in silky clouds. Soon Molly was dipping hot water from the large tub, pouring it into a smaller tub in which her mother vigorously scrubbed clothing on a washboard.

Both women had honey-blond hair, but Betty's was pinned in an upsweep on top of her head, while her daughter's dangled loosely to her shoulders. As Molly poured additional hot water into the smaller tub, Betty paused long enough to elbow perspiration from her forehead and blow an unruly wisp of hair from her eyes.

Mother and daughter were identical in size, both standing four inches over five feet, with slender, well-proportioned figures. Their facial features were similar, though Betty conceded that Molly was better looking. While people said Betty was pretty, they spoke of Molly as being strikingly beautiful. The nineteen-year-old woman disdained the thought, however, insisting that whatever looks she might have, they came from her lovely mother.

"Need some more water, honey," Betty said as she

continued to scrub hard on a shirt. "The hotter the better. I declare, your father must search around that blacksmith shop for dirt to rub into his shirts."

Molly chuckled. "Men are like that, aren't they? Even when they're little boys. Remember how Bobby used to find dirt in places where there *was* no dirt?"

At the mention of her dead son, Betty's face took on a wistful look. "How could I forget? Bobby was so much like your father. If he were alive now, he would probably be as tall, too."

Molly plunged her empty bucket into the hot water and said, "We all still miss Bobby."

"Mm-hmm. Though time has taken away the sharpness of the pain, I still find myself wondering what he would be like today."

Molly poured in more hot water as her mother dropped the clean shirt into a tub of cool water for rinsing. Betty picked up another dirty shirt and dipped it into the hot soapy brew. Scrubbing the shirt energetically against the ribs of the washboard, she said, "I'll tell you, I'd rather be washing these greasy, sooty shirts than worrying over your father like I used to."

Molly smiled. "Anything would be better than living the way we did then. Seeing Daddy only once a month or so . . . always wondering if he was going to get shot in a holdup, or be run down and captured or killed by some lawman somewhere . . . I'm glad those awful days are over."

"Life has been wonderful here in Buffalo these past two years," commented Betty. "I'd forgotten what real happiness was all about."

Molly set down her bucket and began rinsing out the shirt that had just gone into the cool water. "It does me so much good to see you this happy, Mother," she said with a twinkle in her blue eyes.

Betty squeezed her daughter around the shoulders,

smiled, and nodded. "Things are better than they have been since before the drought hit us in Colorado."

As they returned to their work, Molly said, "I just hope that when I get married my husband will be as responsible and considerate as Daddy is now."

Betty stopped her scrubbing and arched her eyebrows. "When you get married? Is there some young man that I don't know about?"

Smiling, the young blond woman said, "There's no one yet."

"Well," observed Betty, "there certainly are some fine young men in and around Buffalo. There's Dan Landess at the general store . . . Harold Benton at the bank . . . and that cowboy from the Diamond M ranch, Matt Yarrow. And all of them seem to have eyes for you."

Molly's face flushed. "I don't know about that, Mother."

"I do," said Betty, wringing soapy water from the shirt in her hands. "And then there's that cowboy from the Bar S. You know—Gus Leonard's friend. The one that's so good-looking."

Molly's blue eyes seemed to light up. Trying to cover the lilt she felt inside, she said nonchalantly, "Oh, you mean Larry Mangrum."

"Ah, that's his name. With that square-cut face of his, he makes me think of a Greek god. And, oh, that black curly hair!"

"Really, Mother!" Molly exclaimed. "If I didn't know better, I'd think you were the one who is nineteen and single!"

Betty laughed as she lowered the soapy shirt into the tub with the cool water. "Well, honey, Larry Mangrum thinks you are something to look at. I've seen him casting glances at you many times. Have you two ever done more than say hello to each other in town?"

"Not really," replied Molly. "And I think you're exaggerating. Larry's friendly, but I don't think he sees me as anyone special."

"I know what I've observed," Betty said flatly. "I think I'll talk to Gus and see if we can't arrange a meeting for you two."

"Mother, don't you dare!" blurted the young blonde.

"He just seems a little shy," Betty continued. "Maybe a little help—"

"You heard me, Mother!" Molly laughed playfully. "Don't you dare meddle!"

Betty was echoing her daughter's laugh as Molly finished wringing out the shirt in her hands and turned to hang it on the clothesline. But the young woman suddenly froze as she saw two men round the corner of the house. In spite of the summer heat, she broke into a cold sweat, and her heart seemed to turn to ice. The stout man walking beside Sheriff Glenn Watkins was the U.S. marshal who had been on her father's trail for so long.

From the side of her mouth, Molly gasped over her shoulder, "Mother!"

The tone of her daughter's voice brought Betty's head around, and her eyes focused on the two men. As she recognized John Claxton, she drew a quick intake of breath, and every nerve in her body went as tight as a fiddle string. It was as if Molly and her talking about how content they now were had brought the federal man on the scene.

Betty's face was white and strained, and her wet hands were tightly clenched as the two lawmen approached.

"Betty . . . Molly," said Watkins. "I guess you remember Marshal John Claxton."

Before either could respond, Claxton touched the brim of his hat and said, "Good morning, ladies. I haven't seen you since Denver."

Both women were numb, knowing that the marshal's presence along with the sheriff meant he knew the whereabouts of Pete Wells.

Looking directly at Betty, Watkins said in as soft a tone as he could manage, "Betty, I sure hate to tell you this, but you've got to know. I have your husband in custody. He's locked up in the jail."

Betty's knees went rubbery, and Molly dashed to her just ahead of Glenn Watkins, who did the same. Taking hold of her mother with firm hands, Molly guided her to the porch of the house and sat her down on a straight-backed wooden chair. Betty's eyes were wide, and her hand was at her throat. Molly kept a grip on her with one hand while she looked at the sheriff and gestured toward a water bucket with the other. Watkins got the message. Hurriedly he went to the bucket, lifted the ladle, and carried it to Betty, placing it to her colorless lips.

John Claxton waited until Betty seemed in control of herself before saying, "Mrs. Wells, I am taking your husband to Rawlins on tomorrow's stage. He will stand trial there for his crimes. I think it is reasonable to assume the jury will convict him. He will be incarcerated in the territorial prison at Rawlins for whatever sentence the judge gives him."

Losing her composure, Betty Wells broke into incoherent sobs. Glenn Watkins attempted to help Molly in quieting her down, but Molly waved him off and then gripped her mother firmly by the shoulders. Speaking in a level tone, she spent several minutes getting her mother's attention and calming her down. The two lawmen eyed each other helplessly.

As Betty's sobs began to abate, Molly said, "Mother, listen to me. We don't know how long Daddy's sentence will be, but there is no reason that we can't move to Rawlins so we can be close to him. We can visit him often."

Betty's eyes lit up. "Yes! And you and I . . . we'll find a way to make a living, honey. At least we'll be able to see your father as often as the prison officials will let us."

Sheriff Glenn Watkins moved close and said, "Maybe I should tell you, Betty. When we took Fred into custody, he asked me to see that the two of you were taken care of.

J. D. Ryle offered to give financial help, and since then many others have said they would do the same thing—myself included. If you stay here in Buffalo, you won't have to worry about making a living."

Betty Wells was touched by the generosity of Buffalo's citizens. With a tremor in her voice, she said, "Sheriff Watkins, I—I am overwhelmed to say the least." She sniffed, wiping her eyes with a handkerchief. "But Molly and I have to be as close to my husband as possible. We'll find a way to care for ourselves in Rawlins. Besides, it wouldn't be right for us to take money from our friends. I hope you understand, and I hope the others will, too."

"Yes, ma'am." Watkins nodded. "I understand."

Having regained her composure, Betty stood up and said to the sheriff, "I want to see my husband now. Is that all right?"

"That will be fine, ma'am," replied Watkins. "The marshal and I will escort you to the jail."

Twenty minutes later the two women were making their way down the street accompanied by Watkins and Claxton. As they drew near the sheriff's office, a large group of townspeople was returning to the street from the alley behind the jail. Upon seeing Betty and Molly, they formed a huge circle around them, speaking words of comfort and encouragement.

J. D. Ryle elbowed his way through the crowd to the two women, also making a path for the Reverend Wallace Perkins. Ryle said, "Betty, we've just come from seeing your husband, and he told us the whole story. We're so sorry to hear about all your trouble. Like we told Fred, we can understand why he was driven to do what he did. Now you listen. We told Fred that we all want to do whatever we can to help you and Molly—and we mean it."

"That's right," the Reverend Perkins said. "Your church will stand behind you, Mrs. Sheridan."

Ryle spoke again. "Also, I want you to know, Betty, I

told Fred that if I'm still in business when he gets out of prison, he has a job waiting for him."

Her eyes glistening with tears, Betty said falteringly, "J.D., you've been so kind to us. . . . My husband has never been happier than he's been working for you. And Pastor Perkins, I want you and everyone else to know how much we appreciate your friendship . . . and your generous offers of help." She looked at Molly and took her hand. "But Molly and I feel that we should be near my husband—especially now when he needs us so much. So . . . we're going to move to Rawlins."

Assured by her many friends that they understood, Betty led her daughter toward the jail and entered, followed by the two lawmen. Unlocking the door between the office and the cell area, Watkins said, "Fred is the only prisoner in the jail at present, ladies. I'll let you go back alone so you can have some privacy. Just rap on the door when you're ready to leave."

Mother and daughter stepped through the door and heard it lock behind them. When they reached the cell area, Pete leaped from the bunk where he had been sitting and extended his arms through the bars. He embraced his wife and daughter as the three of them wept together.

It was late in the afternoon, and Bill Owens had just finished giving Betty Wells two tickets on the next day's stage, compliments of the stage line, when Marshal Claxton barreled into the office, a sour look on his face. Touching his hatbrim, he said, "Ma'am, I really don't think it's a good idea for you and the girl to travel on the stage tomorrow when I am taking your husband in as a prisoner."

"Why not?" Betty snapped. Her nerves were already pulled tight from the strain of her husband's arrest, and now this man was saying she should not go with him. The marshal, she felt, was treading on ground where he did not belong.

Claxton cleared his throat nervously and replied, "I just don't like the idea."

"Why? I don't understand."

"Uh . . . well, ma'am, I'm—"

"What about other passengers booked on the stage, Marshal? Are you going to put *them* off?" Fire was flaring in Betty's blue eyes, and her brows were furrowed with anger.

"Well, no, ma'am. I wouldn't do that, but—"

"But what?" Betty cut in. "Aren't you really saying that you don't want us on the stage because you're afraid we'll hit you on the head or something so we can free Pete?"

The marshal's lips pulled into a thin line. Before he could answer, the irate woman clipped, "Well, relax, sir. We promise not to cause you any grief—and Pete won't give you any trouble, either."

"Listen, ma'am," said Claxton. "I would just rather—"

"No, Marshal," she said. "I have the tickets right here, given us by the generosity of Mr. Ross Blake. Molly and I are sticking by my husband. We are going on the stage with him." With that, Betty headed out the door of the office, Molly trailing behind.

The marshal was left standing there, his mouth hanging open.

As Jack Parris walked his horse down Main Street, he pulled his hat low. His face was known by men all over these parts, and he did not want his plan to be spoiled by having someone on the street recognize him. Though he had been through Buffalo on many occasions—usually to visit Willie Hooks—he had never met Johnson County's sheriff, Glenn Watkins. Smiling to himself, he thought, *Well, that is going to change shortly. I'll soon have a nice present for Sheriff Watkins—and he can wire Rawlins for my money.*

When the blacksmith shop came into view, Parris pulled out the poster and studied the face of Pete Wells. He replaced it in his pocket as he shifted his gaze from boardwalk to boardwalk along the street to see if anyone was taking note of his presence. No one was paying him any attention. As he passed the sheriff's office, he thought, *See you in a few minutes, Watkins.*

Reining in at the blacksmith shop, Parris could hear within the deep wheeze of the bellows and the ring of a hammer. Dismounting, he glanced in both directions along the street. People were milling about, but no one was approaching on his side of the street. Pushing his hat back slightly, he stepped into the shop, his eyes quickly focusing on the short, stout man at the fire pit. Having memorized the photograph on the poster, he knew this was not the fugitive.

His gaze quickly raked the building, but no one else was visible. At that moment the short man noticed him and stopped his hammering.

"Howdy, mister," he said pleasantly in greeting. "What can I do for you?"

"I'm, uh . . . looking for Fred Sheridan," the bounty hunter replied.

The blacksmith's round face stiffened. "He isn't here."

"When will he be back?"

"You a friend of his?"

"Uh . . . no. Not exactly. I, uh . . . my horse has a shoe that keeps working loose, and Sheridan was recommended to me by a friend. Since I was passing through town I thought I'd have him look at it."

Moving closer, the blacksmith said in an amiable tone, "I can take a look at it for you."

Parris snickered nervously. "No offense, sir, but my friend told me not to let anybody touch it but Fred Sheridan. Said Fred can make a shoe fit a horse like nobody else can."

The short man looked a bit puzzled as he said, "I'm mighty pleased to hear that Fred has customers who feel that way about him, but if you want the shoe attended to, it'll have to be me that does it. Fred won't be around for a while."

"Well, I can wait," countered the bounty hunter. "How about if I come back later?"

Suddenly the blacksmith's eyes were full of shadow. "Might be twenty years," he said with a tremor to his voice.

Jack Parris was not sure he had heard correctly. "Did you say *twenty years?*"

"Yes. Fred was arrested by a U.S. marshal earlier today. The marshal says he's a wanted man, an outlaw. His real name is Pete Wells."

The words hit Jack Parris like a battering ram in the belly. He tried to cover the effect of the jolt, but his face instantly turned to putty. In his mind he pictured the five thousand dollars flying away like an elusive eagle, headed for lofty heights and forever out of reach.

He turned slightly, trying to hide his features from the blacksmith, and made an effort to adopt his original expression. Then, acting as if he were taking in items of interest in the shop, he said, "That's too bad."

"Yeah." The blacksmith nodded. "He's worked for me for two years. Never had a man who was so good at his work, on top of being totally reliable."

The bounty hunter, his features again under control, looked at the owner and said, "Well, I guess that just goes to show. My pa used to say that you never really know anybody. Not even yourself."

Shaking his head, the blacksmith said, "I sure thought I knew Fred Sheridan. Such a nice fella. Family man and all. Just never dreamed— Oh, well, no sense moaning over it. Do you want me to take a look at the shoe?"

"Uh . . . no, it's really not that bad. I'll have it checked some other time. Sorry to have bothered you."

"No bother," the shop owner said to Jack Parris's back as he disappeared through the large doorway.

Anger and disappointment flowed in a fiery mixture through the bounty hunter. He was a day too late. If only Willie Hooks had made his discovery one day sooner . . . Swearing under his breath, Parris looked up and down the street for the nearest saloon. The only thing he could do now was tie on a drunk. When he sobered up, he would go bear the bad news to Willie and head elsewhere.

The newly painted sign of the Red Dog Saloon caught Parris's eye, and he led his horse down the street, still swearing under his breath. Tying the animal to the hitch rail, he stomped across the boardwalk and shouldered his way through the batwings.

He was surprised to see so many customers in the saloon at this hour. The sun had just touched the tops of the Bighorn Mountains to the west of town. Approaching the bar, he hooked his right foot on the brass rail and ordered a double shot of whiskey. He downed it in two gulps and asked for another of the same.

The second one he took slower, leaning on the bar with an elbow while sipping the fiery liquid, lamenting the loss of the five thousand dollars. Then something that was being said in conversation by a group of men seated around two adjacent tables against the far wall caught his attention. He was sure he had heard the name Pete Wells.

The mood of the men seemed subdued. They were speaking in low tones, and Parris could not make out every word. Asking the bartender for a bottle, he plunked down the money and carried it, along with his shot glass, to a table near the spot where the group was seated. A few eyes picked up his presence, but Parris acted uninterested as he eased into a chair with his back to them.

The conversation continued. One voice seemed to dominate the discussion, and Parris, listening closely, learned that the man's name was Ross Blake. He seemed to know a lot about the stagecoach that was due in the next day.

A voice in the group said, "How come he's doin' it that way, Ross?"

"Yeah," piped up another. "What's he gonna do with his horse? Tie it to the back of the stage?"

"I can't let him do that," came Blake's reply. "His horse could never maintain the pace we set, what with a fresh stage team waiting for us at every way station. Guess he'll leave it here and pick it up some other time."

Another voice said, "We all know Fred—I mean, Pete—isn't dangerous. But Claxton thinks he is. If Pete were the deadly menace Claxton makes him out to be, wouldn't it be puttin' the other passengers in a bad spot to be ridin' with them?"

"Seems to me it would," acknowledged the man called Blake. "Most lawmen would take him to Rawlins on horseback. But he bought two tickets, and there's no way I could refuse them seats. Pete's wife and daughter are going along. The only other passenger so far is one of the cowhands from the Bar S. When he comes in to board the stage tomorrow, I'll have to advise him that a prisoner is aboard. Give him an opportunity to wait for the next stage if he wishes."

Jack Parris's heart was pounding like a trip-hammer in his breast. Pete Wells was going to be transported to Rawlins by stagecoach! The five thousand dollars might not have eluded him after all. An idea was quickly forming in his brain. Suddenly he decided he was not going to get drunk. He had other things to do. There was one more seat left on tomorrow's stage to Rawlins . . . and it was going to be his.

Jack Parris was about to rise from the table and make his way to the batwings when two angry-looking men rumbled through the door. They did a quick survey of the place and then turned toward the group assembled at the far wall. The larger of the two led the way in that direction, flinging chairs and overturning tables that stood in his way.

The bartender hastily took up pursuit after them. As he came up behind them, swearing at the top of his voice, every man in the place was watching the scene.

The larger of the two angry men turned and pointed a stiff finger at the bartender. "You stay where you are, barkeep!" he boomed, murder in his eyes. "We've got business with Ross Blake, and you ain't gonna interfere!"

The bartender pulled to a halt, fear transforming his face. By this time, Ross Blake was on his feet, looking the larger man square in the eye. He seemed to recognize both men.

"What are you two doing here?" Blake asked. "You were on the stage to Great Falls—the names are Boyd and Mann, right?"

"*Were* on the stage is right, Blake!" blustered the smaller one. "That driver and shotgunner of yours put us off thirty miles out!"

The angular features of the owner of the stage line seemed to stiffen. "They must have had good reason, Boyd."

"Good reason? Bah!" the other man spit. "There ain't no good rea—"

"Were you drinking?" cut in Blake.

"So what if we were?"

"I have rules on my stages. No drinking, and if there are women aboard, no smoking."

"Yeah," Boyd spoke up, moving up beside his friend. "That's what your driver told us. Well, we don't like them rules."

"You knew the rules before you boarded," Blake replied coldly, his brown eyes hardening with determination.

"We had to walk back!" hissed Mann. "We want our money back, or else!"

Anger instantly darkened Blake's face. Squaring his broad shoulders, he rasped, "Or else what?"

"Or else I'm gonna take it out of your stinkin' hide!" the one called Mann threatened.

Parris watched as one of the men seated at Blake's table stood up and said, "Now, look, mister. You—"

But Blake silenced him with the wave of a hand. Through his teeth he growled, "You two broke the rules. You've got no refunds coming. Now clear out of here."

The smell of a fight was building in the smoke-filled room. Mann was breathing like a mad beast as Boyd stood next to him, ready to make his move a split second after his friend did.

Then, with the swiftness of a weaver's shuttle, Blake's booted foot lashed out and caught Boyd savagely in the belly. While Boyd was doubled over, Blake unleashed a hissing punch, his iron-hard fist connecting with Mann's jaw, literally lifting the big brute off his feet. Mann sailed three yards before crashing into a table, splintering the legs and smashing the tabletop flat to the floor. He lay sprawled on it, out cold.

For a moment a deep silence came over the saloon. Then the silence was broken by Boyd, who lay on the floor, groaning in pain and giving up whatever was in his stomach.

Jack Parris took advantage of the moment to glide toward the batwings and slip outside unnoticed. Pulling his hat low, he swung into the saddle and guided his horse up the street. The scene he had just witnessed played itself over again in his mind. He marveled that Mann's head was still attached to his body. When Blake's fist met its mark with such force, Parris had expected to see the head come flying off. He had seen many a fight in his day, but never had he seen anyone punch like Ross Blake. He shuddered at the thought of ever having to meet the man in a fistfight.

With his new plan well concocted, the bounty hunter entered a clothing store in the next block just before closing time and spent most of what money he had left on an expensive business suit, shirt, string tie, boots, and Stetson hat, reserving the money he would need to purchase the stage ticket. A quarter of an hour later he was passing through the door of Willie Hooks's shack.

As Jack Parris laid out his new outfit on the kitchen table, Willie looked at him askance and asked, "What in thunder is goin' on, Jack?"

Parris explained that a U.S. marshal had that very day arrested Pete Wells and was taking him to Rawlins on the noon stage tomorrow. "At first I thought we'd lost our chance at the big money, Willie," he continued, "but I've figured out a way to get it."

"Whatcha gonna do?" the old man asked, scratching at his scaly scalp.

"I'm going to shave and bathe, and you're going to give me a haircut. There's one seat left on that stage, and I'm going to be on it, wearing these fancy duds and disguised as a successful businessman from over in Gilette. The marshal's name is Claxton. We met once a few years ago, but I don't think he'll recognize me all spruced up. At some point during the trip I'll find a way to get rid of Claxton without the others knowing about it. Then I'll take Wells as my prisoner. I'll make it look like Wells killed Claxton in order to escape. Then I'll say that I recaptured Wells and am bringing him in for the reward!"

"Whew! Sounds all right if you can work it that way, Jack," said Willie. "But what if that exactly right opportunity don't present itself?"

Setting his jaw, Parris replied, "Then I'll just have to kill everybody on the stage. I'll kill Wells, too, and take his body into Rawlins. I'll tell the authorities that Wells went berserk and shot everybody in an attempt to escape, and I was the only one he couldn't kill. Nobody will be able to prove any different."

Willie grinned maliciously. "Then I guess I'm gonna get my thousand dollars no matter what!"

"That's right," said Parris. "I'll leave my horse here with

you. When I come back to get it, I'll have your money in my hand."

Two hours later, Jack Parris knocked on the door of Bill Owens's living quarters above the stage-line office and introduced himself as Ray Thompson, a businessman from Gilette. He bought a ticket for the remaining seat on the stage and headed back to Willie's shack, where he planned to sleep outside on the porch.

But the anticipation of getting his hands on the reward money kept him wide awake. Nothing was going to stand in the way of his collecting that five thousand dollars . . . nothing.

Chapter Four

Just before noon the next day, Jack Parris appeared at the door of the Buffalo Stage Line. Bill Owens looked up from where he was bent over the counter and smiled. "Howdy, Mr. Thompson. Other than being like the southern tip of Hades, it's a nice day, isn't it?"

"Yeah." Feeling strange without his long hair and beard, the bounty hunter nodded. "I like winter better than summer."

Owens chuckled. "Well, I can't say I'm wild about Wyoming winters. I'd take spring weather the year round if I had my choice."

"Stage going to leave on time?" Parris asked.

"Should," replied Owens. "Oughta be getting in any minute now."

At that moment the impressive shadow of Ross Blake filled the doorway. As Blake entered, Owens said, "Ross, I'd like you to meet Mr. Ray Thompson. He's riding the Rawlins stage today."

Blake offered his hand, and Parris felt the steel grip and thought of the scene he had witnessed the day before at the Red Dog. He was relieved that the big man did not recognize him after being in the saloon the day before, but with his fancy clothes and haircut he was not too surprised.

Blake released Parris's hand and said to Owens, "Bill, did you tell Mr. Thompson about the marshal and Pete Wells?"

"Sure did," Owens said. "Told him last night when he bought the ticket. Says it won't bother him none."

"That's right," volunteered Parris.

Blake nodded and then said to Owens, "We've got a problem, Bill. Mrs. Darnell was on my doorstep at dawn this morning to tell me that Nate is down with grippe. Doc Cummins says he won't be driving the stage for at least a week."

Owens ran a hand over his mouth. "What are we gonna do?"

"Well, it looks like—"

Blake was interrupted as his redheaded shotgunner, Hal Stacy, burst through the door. Stacy, a lean, small man in his early twenties, said, "Boss, I just saw Doc Cummins on the street, and he told me about Nate. I know I'm new in the business, but I'll take a stab at driving if you can find me a man to ride shotgun."

"I appreciate the offer, Hal," said Blake, "but there has to be an experienced man at the reins. I was just about to tell Bill that I'll drive this run myself."

Owens said, "If I know Bert Kinney, Ross, he'll offer to turn right around and drive the stage back to Rawlins."

"Probably," agreed Blake. "But there's no way he can do it. He's got to have his rest. There's no reason I can't do it, so that's the way it will be. Hal, you'll ride shotgun with me instead of Nate."

"Okay," said Stacy, turning toward the door. "I need to run over to the general store for a minute. See you shortly."

"Before you leave," spoke up Bill Owens, "shake hands with Mr. Ray Thompson. He'll be riding with you on this trip."

Stacy shook hands with the man and then said to Blake, "Be back in a few minutes."

Blake nodded and moved behind the counter. As he

and Owens engaged in conversation, Parris quietly moved outside and stood in the shade of the canopy that hung over the front of the building. People were bustling on the street amid the wagons and buggies that were passing by. Parris was thinking about the way Ross Blake had handled the two angry men at the Red Dog, and he was none too happy knowing that the hard-muscled owner of the stage line would be driving the run to Rawlins. But then he brightened, reasoning that Blake had no reason to be watching a man dressed in a suit. The right moment would present itself, and Parris would get his bounty.

Momentarily two riders came into the bounty hunter's view and pulled up in front of the stage office. Their horses bore the Bar S brand. The tall, slender one had a small valise tied behind his saddle. He dismounted, handed the reins to the other man, and then untied the valise. Parris noted that though the man on the ground had the unmistakable cut of a cowhand, he wore a Colt .45 on his right hip, its holster thonged to his slender thigh. Putting the valise in his left hand, the one with the Colt shook hands with the other cowboy. There were a few quiet words of parting between them, and then the one on the ground said audibly, "Take care, Gus."

The one named Gus nodded, a solemn look on his face, and then rode away, leading the other horse behind him. When the lanky cowhand stepped into the shade of the canopy, Jack Parris etched a friendly look on his sharp-featured face and said, "You going on the Rawlins stage?"

"Yes." The cowboy nodded. "You, too?"

"Yeah."

"My name's Larry Mangrum," he said, extending his hand.

Meeting it, Jack Parris lied, "Mine's Ray Thompson."

"Looks like it'll be a hot, dusty one," commented the cowboy.

"You're right about that." Parris grinned, adjusting his holster. He was not used to wearing it high on his waist.

At that moment he caught sight of movement on the boardwalk in front of the jail. U.S. Marshal John Claxton was walking beside Pete Wells, whose hands were cuffed in front of him. Behind them were two fair-haired women.

Larry Mangrum said, "What the devil—" He was surprised to see Fred Sheridan in handcuffs. Then he noticed that both Molly Sheridan and her mother were following Fred and the big lawman who escorted him. Larry felt excitement building within him as Molly drew near. Her singular beauty had captivated him since they first met nearly six months ago. Each time they had seen each other since then, she had unknowingly implanted herself deeper in his thoughts. He had hoped to get to know her better one day.

As the procession drew near, a cold feeling washed over Larry Mangrum. He was going home to face one of the West's fastest gunmen. He would never see Molly Sheridan again.

Looking beyond the two men, Larry marveled at how much Molly looked like her mother. Though Molly's features were quite solemn, when her soft glance touched Mangrum, she afforded him a warm smile. Feeling the pull of that smile, as he always did, he felt his heart race.

Larry happened to glance at Ray Thompson at that moment and frowned when he saw the way the man was eyeing Molly and her mother, looking them up and down. Then Thompson looked at the U.S. marshal and seemed to stiffen. Larry wondered what the man had to hide.

At that moment Hal Stacy passed behind Larry and Thompson to go into the stage-line office. He almost bumped his boss, who was just coming out the door. Ross Blake approached the cowhand and said, "You're Larry Mangrum, aren't you?"

"Yes." Larry smiled.

"I'm Ross Blake, owner of the stage line, and there's something I need to tell you about this run."

Blake's attempt to explain to his passenger that an outlaw in handcuffs would be riding the Rawlins stage was interrupted by the booming voice of John Claxton as the group drew near. "How come the stage isn't in yet, Blake?"

"I don't rightly know. But it's just now twelve o'clock, so it should be pulling in any minute."

"Seems to me," said Claxton, "if it was to leave at twelve, it should have been in here at least fifteen or twenty minutes ago."

As the marshal spoke, Bill Owens and Hal Stacy came through the office door carrying one of the Wells family's trunks. They set it on the edge of the boardwalk and went back after the other one.

"Like I said," Blake replied to Claxton, "it should be pulling in any minute. Now if you'll excuse me, I need to help my boys bring the luggage from the office so we can load the stage fast when it gets here."

Claxton set his steady eyes on the bounty hunter and the cowboy.

"You two going on the stage?"

They both nodded.

"Blake and Owens tell you that you'll be riding with outlaw Pete Wells here? I'm taking him to Rawlins to stand trial."

"Blake told me," said Parris.

Larry Mangrum's brow furrowed. There was concern in his eyes. "Pardon me, Marshal," he said, "but this man is Fred Sheridan. I know him. He has put shoes on my horse."

At that moment, Ross Blake came out carrying several pieces of luggage, followed by his two men, bearing the second trunk that belonged to the Wells family. Having heard Larry's words, Blake suddenly realized he had not finished explaining the situation to him. Molly and her mother gave each other a pained look as the words came from Blake's mouth. "His name is really Pete Wells, Mangrum. He's a wanted criminal. I was going to tell you about it but didn't get the chance."

"If you think you're in any danger, son," put in Claxton, "you can take a later stage."

Larry Mangrum's attention was now on Molly Wells, whose face was flushed with embarrassment. "I had to tell you my last name was Sheridan," she said shyly. "But my first name really is Molly."

Overwhelmed by her beauty, Larry replied, "That's all right, Miss Molly. It's . . . it's just that this takes me by surprise." Swinging his gaze to Wells, he said, "You just don't seem the type. You sure are a mighty good blacksmith."

"It's a long story, Larry," said Wells.

"Guess I'll get a chance to hear it." Larry grinned. "We've got a lengthy trip ahead."

Owens and Stacy had returned to the office and were now setting down a heavy wooden crate marked Firearms. They hurried back through the door to bring out other freight, including a wooden box bearing ammunition for the rifles.

Larry Mangrum was once again looking at Molly when John Claxton asked the clean-shaven man in the business suit, "What's your name, mister?"

Feeling the pressure of the lawman's scrutinizing eyes on him, the bounty hunter answered, "Name's Ray Thompson, Marshal. I'm from Gilette."

Turning to the cowhand, Claxton said, "And you, son? I heard Mr. Blake call you Mangrum. What's your first name?"

"Larry, sir."

Taking in the tied-down holster with a quick glance, Claxton asked, "You a gunfighter?"

"No, sir. I'm a ranch hand at the Bar S, west of town."

"Seems to me it's gunslicks who wear their guns tied down, not cowboys."

Larry could feel Molly's eyes on him. Now it was his turn to be embarrassed. He hoped she would not think less of him when she learned the truth that was about to come from his lips. In a level tone he said to Claxton, "I used to be a gunfighter, Marshal. I saw the foolishness of it and gave it up. I am now a ranch hand, and I tie my holster down simply because I feel more comfortable with it this way."

Claxton did not comment. He turned back to Parris and said, "What line of business you in, Thompson?"

The lawman's penetrating eyes seemed to make the other man nervous. "I'm in real estate," he replied quickly. "On my way to Rawlins to close a deal."

The marshal rubbed his chin, squinting at the thin man, who did not seem at ease in the clothes he was wearing. Claxton cocked his head sideways, squinted deeper, and said, "Have we met somewhere before?"

Holding his voice steady, he said, "Not that I recall, Marshal."

"You say you're from Gilette?"

The bounty hunter worked hard at covering his nervousness. He had to make his masquerade work. "Yes," he responded. "Some friends brought me to Buffalo, since they had to make the trip anyhow."

Claxton seemed satisfied. He looked up the street and said to Blake, "What do you suppose is keeping that stage?"

"I don't know, Marshal," said the tall man, "but since it hasn't come yet, why don't all of you come into the office and sit down?"

The passengers filed in and sat on wooden chairs. They made light conversation, diverting their thoughts from the tardiness of the stagecoach.

By one o'clock there was still no stage in sight. Outside on the boardwalk Ross Blake, Bill Owens, and Hal Stacy paced nervously beside the stack of freight and luggage. Wringing his hands, Blake said, "Fellas, I'm afraid some of the renegade Sioux have attacked the stage."

Stacy said, "We've been lucky so far, boss. I've been expecting to see those redskinned devils coming at us any time now."

Owens rubbed the back of his neck. "I sure hope it isn't Two Thumbs. If he's come down from Montana to wreak havoc on us in Wyoming, we're in for it. If he has waylaid the stage, we'll probably never see it again—or the crew, passengers, and horses."

While Blake and his two men were discussing the possible fate of the late stagecoach, the passengers inside the office were getting edgy. Marshal Claxton left his chair and walked to the door, looked out, and saw Blake and the others and still no stage. Swearing under his breath, he returned to the chair.

Larry Mangrum and Molly Wells were sitting next to each other, engaged in conversation. They were talking about their childhood days and of happy occasions they treasured in memory. Molly was surprised to learn that Larry's father was a Baptist minister. When she began to ask questions about how he had become a gunfighter and why he had given it up, Larry steered the conversation to Molly and her family.

The lovely blonde soon found herself telling Larry about her deceased brother and of the events that led up to his untimely death. From there the line of conversation eventually arrived at the inevitable subject . . . her father's reason for becoming an outlaw.

Pete and Betty Wells sat in silence, holding hands, as their daughter quietly began to tell the story of her father's outlawry to the young man. Feeling for his daughter, Wells cut in on the conversation and said, "Larry, as long as we have time right now, let me tell you the story."

"Sure. I'm eager to hear it."

Within twenty minutes Pete Wells had finished.

"I never would have dreamed it of you, sir," Larry commented, "but at least I'm glad you decided to go straight. And I'm so glad Mrs. Wells and Molly can move to Rawlins to be near you. It will help the time go faster if you can see them often."

Molly said, "Larry, are going home to Rawlins just to visit?"

"Uh . . . no, Miss Molly," he replied. "I quit my job at the Bar S. I'm, uh . . . going back to Rawlins on a permanent basis." The black-haired cowhand was a bit off balance by Molly's probing of this subject. He did not want her to know about his pending shootout with Vic Spain. She would never understand, and she would probably look down on him as a fool.

"Permanently?" she reacted, seeming quite pleased. "That's good! Maybe we will see each other from time to time. Do you have a job waiting for you there?"

Larry was trying to find a diplomatic way to lie about his situation when he saw Bill Owens appear at the door.

"Hey, everybody!" Owens called. "The stage is coming!"

Larry looked up at the clock on the office wall as he stood up. It was twenty minutes after two. The group filed through the office door onto the boardwalk, Claxton staying close to Pete Wells. Larry was relieved that, at least for the moment, he did not have to confess the truth to Molly. He was certain she would think less of him when she learned it.

The tardy stagecoach was still at the far end of the street, and as it drew closer, Blake, Owens, and Stacy noted that young Phil Hartman, the shotgunner, was driving, and an unidentified man was holding the shotgun in the seat next to him. Bert Kinney, the regular driver, was not in sight. Blake and his two men looked at each other with concern and then turned their attention back to the coach as it rolled in and stopped amid a cloud of dust.

The afternoon breeze carried the dust away as Ross Blake stepped up quickly and said, "Phil, where's Bert? What's happened?"

Phil Hartman quickly told his employer that Kinney was inside the coach with a broken ankle. Twenty miles back, he explained, the rear axle had been acting up. Upon inspection, they found that the four bolts that held it to the frame had worked loose. Bert Kinney had slid underneath the coach to tighten them, and as he was doing so, a jackrabbit spooked the horses. Bert's ankles were in line with the rear wheel on the right side of the vehicle, and when the horses jumped, the coach jerked forward in spite of the tightened brake. The wheel rolled over Kinney's right ankle and broke it. After they had splinted the ankle, one of the male passengers had volunteered to ride shotgun.

Hal Stacy and Phil Hartman helped Bert Kinney down from the stage, and two bystanders on the street were enlisted to carry him into the doctor's office. While the passengers alighted, Ross Blake thanked the man who had ridden shotgun, relieved that the delay of his stagecoach had not been caused by Indians.

As Owens and Stacy unloaded the luggage, with some help from Larry Mangrum, Phil Hartman looked around the area and asked Blake, "Where's George?"

"Down with the grippe," Blake replied flatly.

Hartman lifted his hat, sleeving away sweat, and said, "That leaves you without a driver. Bert can't do it. You want me to take it?"

"No," said Blake. "Hal offered, too, but I'd prefer—"

Marshal Claxton, who had apparently been listening to the conversation, butted in, saying, "Blake, you've got to see that the stage goes to Rawlins. You aren't thinking of canceling this run, are you?"

"No," responded Blake. "The run must be made. We have a crate of rifles, along with ammunition, that needs to be delivered to the people down in Arminto. The town is a bit off our route, but they're having Indian problems and desperately need the weapons. I was about to tell Phil that I am going to drive the stage on this run."

"Good," said the marshal.

"Besides," added Blake, "a cavalry platoon from Fort Fetterman will be waiting at the way station near Deadman Butte at the appointed time. They're going to escort us from there to Rawlins. If the stage doesn't arrive,

they'll think the Sioux attacked it. We've got to get loaded
and be on our way."

Pete Wells, who stood next to the marshal with Betty
beside him, said, "Ross, I'll be glad to help you with the
loading if you can talk the marshal into taking off these
cuffs."

Claxton's head whipped around. He set his harsh glare
on Wells, and then hissing though his teeth, he said,
"Those cuffs are staying on till you're behind bars in
Rawlins, mister!"

The marshal's sharp words roweled Betty, and her face
flushed as she lashed out at him, "Pete is only wanting to
help, Marshal! He isn't going to try to get away from you!"

"Says you!" countered Claxton. "I mean you no personal
offense, ma'am, but I'm wearing the badge here, and your
husband is an outlaw. Just because you and your daughter
are along doesn't change how I am going to handle him.
Like I said, the cuffs stay on."

"Thanks, anyway, Pete," Ross Blake said.

Jack Parris had been quietly observing the scene until
Betty turned to him and said, "Why don't you pitch in and
help, Mr. Thompson? There are no cuffs on your wrists."

Looking a bit sheepish as several eyes fell on him, the
bounty hunter said, "I, uh . . . I have a bad back, ma'am.
Can't do any lifting."

Betty nodded silently, but the look on her face clearly
displayed her doubts as to the veracity of what she had
just heard.

As the men continued to load the luggage and cargo into
the boot and onto the rack, Molly Wells stood near her
mother, casting covert glances at the handsome young
cowhand. When she found Larry looking at her, she swung
her gaze away shyly. When their eyes met a second time,
she gave him a fleeting smile and then quickly looked
away, her cheeks tinting.

John Claxton stepped close to Ross Blake and said,

"Since we've got to swing over to Arminto, what will our route be?"

Blake picked up a stick and stepped into the dusty street. Smoothing out a spot near the edge of the boardwalk with his boot, he roughly sketched a map with the stick. The stage would run due south from Buffalo through the edge of the Bighorn Mountains. The first stop would be Mayoworth. Continuing south, the route would carry the stage just west of the rugged area known as the Hole-in-the-Wall, a rocky canyon where outlaws from all over the West hid from the law. Both Blake and Claxton knew the reputation of the Hole-in-the-Wall. It was certain death for any lawmen who might try to enter its inviolable confines.

The route then angled a bit southwest to a way station near Deadman Butte. The normal course was then to shoot straight south to the town of Waltman, but on this trip the stage would veer a bit southwest to make the delivery of the rifles and ammunition at Arminto. From that point, the stage would pass through Waltman, then head south through Rattlesnake Hills to Muddy Gap. Leaving the way station at Muddy Gap, it would roll out for the last leg of the journey to Rawlins.

Claxton nodded and then asked, "That cavalry platoon you said would meet us at Deadman Butte . . . they coming directly from Fort Fetterman?"

As Blake turned to answer, a deep, rumbling sound met their ears. The other passengers and the crew began to look around for the source of the sound as people on the street swung their heads both ways.

"I'd swear that's a herd of cattle on the move," Claxton observed.

Blake nodded. "Must be running them past the edge of town. Anyway, to answer your question, the platoon is camped near Casper, so they really don't have far to ride to get to Deadman Butte. Another platoon is escorting the northbound stage that is just now pulling out of Rawlins.

The platoon will part with them at the Butte. That leaves us with only eighty miles of the two-hundred-thirty mile run without any protection."

At that instant Hal Stacy's voice cut the air from up top of the stagecoach. "Stampede!"

People were scattering from the street into shops and stores as the loud bawling of cattle was heard above the rumbling of hooves. The thundering herd appeared at the west end of the street, filling its entire breadth. A huge cloud of dust followed the cattle as they came at a run, overturning rainbarrels and shattering chairs and benches along the boardwalk. Riderless horses at the hitch rails were straining at their reins in an attempt to escape the oncoming mass of bawling, sharp-horned, wild-eyed beasts. Teams harnessed to wagons and buggies lurched away from the chaos, their vehicles bounding behind them.

Ross Blake hollered to his passengers and crew, "Get into the office! Hurry!"

Pete Wells cried out for his daughter to get in the building as he picked up his wife in spite of his handcuffs and carried her inside. Larry Mangrum took hold of Molly with a firm grip and pulled her through the door. The others followed, except Hal Stacy, who leaped from the top of the coach into the box and seized the reins. Snapping them at the team of six and shouting at the top of his lungs, he guided the coach down a side street away from the stampede.

The group inside the stage-line office watched through the windows as the frenzied cattle stormed past them in less than two minutes. Miraculously, the stampeding herd had veered around the few pieces of cargo still on the boardwalk, leaving it undamaged. As the dust settled, Blake led the group back out the door. Along the street, people were coming out of the buildings, some inspecting the damage, others looking for their horses.

Sheriff Watkins sprinted through the door of his office as soon as the herd had passed, his gaze sweeping the street as he attempted to see if anyone had been trampled. He spotted two dead saddle horses but no humans lying in the dirt or on the boardwalks. But the herd had left a great deal of property damage in its wake. There was a clamor of voices along the street as people talked excitedly of the incident. The sheriff moved toward the spot where Ross Blake and his group stood in front of the stage-line office, looking for Hal Stacy to return with the stagecoach.

Abruptly a lone rider came galloping down the street, weaving among the clusters of people. When he spied Watkins, he drew rein quickly and skidded his mount to a stop. Watkins recognized him as Len Dobler, the foreman of the Diamond A Ranch, which was located some ten miles north of town.

Remaining in the saddle, Dobler said breathlessly, "Sheriff, if you'll see to it that all damage is reported to my boss, he'll make it good. Anybody hurt that you know of?"

"Don't think so," responded Watkins. "How'd the stampede get started?"

"Two of our big bulls decided to have a dispute just as we were comin' near town. One of them gored the other one real bad. The gored one went wild and started rippin' up those around him, like he'd gone mad or somethin'. Herd went crazy and stampeded right into town. I don't even know where the big brute is at the moment. Lost him in the dust. I don't think he's with the herd."

No sooner had the words left Dobler's mouth than a massive black bull bolted onto the street from between two buildings. The enormous beast had a large, bloody hole in its left side where it had been gored by the other bull. Its eyes bulged insanely as it swung its huge head back and forth, as though trying to decide what to do next. Its sides were heaving, and a bloody foam sprayed from its flared nostrils as it snorted angrily.

Screams and cries of fear resounded along the street as people again began scattering for safety. The titanic beast's sharp, curved horns glistened with crimson. Suddenly the bull's wild eyes focused on an elderly man who was hobbling from the center of the street. The bull roared, took a few steps, then paused and lowered its head for the charge. The old man froze in his tracks about thirty feet from the threatening beast.

Len Dobler saw what was happening and raked his horse's sides, galloping toward the maddened animal. When he skidded his horse to a halt between the bull and the terrified old man, the bull charged. In his fear, the old man took two steps, stumbled, and fell to the ground.

The powerful bull hit Dobler's mount full force, driving its horns deep into the horse's side. With a scream the horse went down, all before Dobler was able to slip from the saddle.

Ross Blake bolted inside the office to get a rifle.

Pete Wells, as if he were sprung from a trap, bounded off the boardwalk and dashed toward the scene. Betty called his name in a half-scream that was choked off as her throat went tight.

Molly and Betty watched in horror as John Claxton whipped out his revolver and shouted for Wells to stop. Instantly Molly screamed at the marshal, "My father's not running away! He's trying to help old Mr. Spangler and that cowhand!"

Claxton gave her a petulant look and then holstered his gun. Molly wrapped her arms around her mother, whose eyes were transfixed on Wells.

Len Dobler's left leg was pinned under the weight of his fallen horse. He sat up but could not move. The bull had delivered the horse a lethal blow, and it was gasping its last few breaths. The bull backed away, blood dripping from its horns. It shook its big, broad head and bellowed with fury; then it began circling Dobler. The ranch foreman was struggling with all his might to free himself before the bull charged, but the dying horse's weight was too great.

Townspeople stood watching from doorways and windows as Pete Wells came to a halt in front of the bull, putting himself between the deadly beast and the helpless cowboy. His voice racketed along the clapboard buildings that lined the street as he faced the bull and waved his shackled hands, shouting, "Hee-yah! Hee-yah!"

The angry bull snorted, spraying bloody foam, and then pawed the soft earth.

Everyone who witnessed the awful scene was mesmerized. Seventy feet away, Betty and Molly Wells stood clinging to each other, as John Claxton, who remained beside them, muttered, "The fool's gonna get himself killed!"

A sudden surge of anger flushed Betty's face. Taking her eyes from her husband, she glared at Claxton as she heatedly snapped, "My husband used to be a cattleman, Marshal! He has handled mad bulls before. You can call him a fool, but he'll show you right now that he's not the outlaw he used to be! He may get gored himself, but he'll do all he can to keep the bull from hurting Len!"

Dobler, from his vulnerable position on the ground, said to Wells, gritting his teeth, "Watch yourself! He'll kill you!"

The crazed beast pawed the ground and shook its head. At that instant, from the corner of his eye, Wells saw Larry Mangrum at his right flank. Directly behind Larry, the old man was struggling to rise. Keeping his eyes on the dangerous brute before him, Wells spoke quietly from the side of his mouth, "Get Mr. Spangler out of here, Larry! Quick!"

Larry was about eight feet from Wells, gun in hand. "How about if I shoot the bull from here, Mr. Wells?" he asked, breathing heavily.

"You can't get a clean shot from where you're standing," Wells gasped. "The bullet has to catch him square between the eyes to kill him with one shot. If you miss the brain, he'll be more dangerous than ever. Hurry! Get Mr. Spangler off the street!"

The young cowhand obeyed instantly. Moving to Spangler, he bent down, cradled the old man's frail body in his arms, and then dashed into the open doorway of the nearest shop. After setting Spangler down, he hurried back to the street as several people rushed to the old man's aid.

Larry saw the bull spray more bloody foam from its nostrils and then charge Pete Wells, bellowing insanely.

Wells braced himself, bent his knees, and leaped away from the deadly horns just in time as the bull hooked at him and rumbled past. The massive animal whirled about, madder than ever. It looked at the helpless man pinned under the horse and then again set its wild gaze on Pete Wells, who was shaking his handcuffed fists and shouting, "Hee-yah! Hee-yah!"

Ross Blake was running along the boardwalk, carrying a Winchester .44. He drew up behind the bull so as to show himself to Pete Wells.

Wells saw Blake lever a cartridge into the chamber just as the bull dug in and charged again.

Again he barely avoided the sharp points of the bull's bloody horns. The enormous beast pivoted while roaring with anger and set itself to charge again.

Ross Blake could not get a clean shot at the bull because Wells was in the way. "Pete!" he called, and when Wells turned, he had already thrown the rifle into the air.

Wells caught the weapon despite his wrists being shackled. He raised the gun to his shoulder and took aim between the eyes of the bull just as it bolted for him. The rifle spat flame, its report clattering along the street. The bull's knees buckled as the slug ripped into its brain, the massive body hitting the street with a loud *thwhump*, raising small clouds of dust. The big animal let out a soft grunt and lay still, its eyes closed in death.

A rousing cheer went up from the townspeople as they

hurried out of the shops and doorways, eager to see to Dobler and the others. Betty Wells ran toward her husband, with Molly on her heels. Claxton was running, his big belly flopping up and down as he headed toward Wells, shouting, "Give me that gun!"

Pete Wells waited until his wife had reached him. Then he grinned at the oncoming marshal and handed the rifle to Ross Blake. After Molly praised her father for his act of heroism, she turned to Larry Mangrum and said, "Thank you, Larry. That was a brave thing you did."

The lanky cowboy's face flushed as he released a wide smile, which Molly then returned. To Larry it was like the sun warming his bones on a cold winter day.

Chapter Five

Marshal John Claxton's beefy face soured as the people of Buffalo heaped praise on Pete Wells for saving Len Dobler's life at the risk of his own. It seemed odd to Claxton that folks could so easily ignore the fact that Pete Wells was an outlaw. *Hmpf*, he thought. *The way they're carrying on, you'd think he was a saint!*

When Len Dobler had been freed from his dead horse and carried to the doctor's office, he expressed his appreciation to Wells for what he had done. Dobler also commended Larry Mangrum and Buffalo's citizens for jumping in to help Wells and for carrying the elderly Mr. Spangler to safety.

It was just past three o'clock when the passengers and crew had settled into the stagecoach and were ready to roll, Ross Blake at the reins. Next to him sat red-haired Hal Stacy, a double-barreled, twelve-gauge shotgun cradled in his arms. In the rack overhead were two big trunks belonging to the Wells family, the large wooden crate containing the rifles, and a wooden box filled with ammunition.

Inside the coach, Pete Wells rode on the front seat, his back to the driver, with his wrists handcuffed to the right doorpost. Each of the three men on the opposite seat—the marshal, Larry, and Jack Parris—held a rifle, Wells being the only man unarmed.

As the townspeople huddled near the coach and bid good-bye to the Wells family, J. D. Ryle stuck his head in the window on Pete Wells's side and said, "Remember what I said, Pete. If I'm still in business when you get out of prison, you've got a job."

"Thanks, J. D.," Wells said with a smile.

"Yes, thank you," said Betty.

"He's gonna get at least twenty years, Ryle," Marshal Claxton cut in. "Judging by your wrinkles and gray hair, I'd say you'll be out of business by then."

Ryle stiffened, pulled his lips into a thin line, and gave the lawman a long, narrow-eyed look. Reaching through the window, he patted the prisoner's shoulder and said, "So long, Pete."

Up in the box, Ross Blake shouted at the team and snapped the reins. The coach lurched and rolled toward the south end of town as the crowd waved them off.

Buffalo soon passed from view while Blake and Stacy sat silently in the box. Blake eyed the location of the sun. It was already on its downward slant into the western sky. He hated to start this late, but it could not be avoided.

Blake let his eyes roam over the country around him. The Bighorn Mountains seemed larger and more alluring than ever. He loved Wyoming. There was something about the broad expanse of blue sky and the vast, endless reaches of the wide-open country that stirred something wild and primitive deep inside him.

He thought of Jenny and how she had loved it here. When she had been alive, they had wandered the countryside on Sunday afternoons, drinking in its vast magnificence. Now his Sunday afternoons were spent at the stage-line office doing paperwork—though he had to admit that much of what he did was unnecessary. But he could not face spending them at home without Jenny.

Blake brought his attention back to the present, glancing at Hal Stacy, seated beside him. Knowing that Indian trouble was possible at any time this far north, the redheaded young man was watching carefully for movement on the land. Blake smiled and then looked ahead of him at the dusty road.

Inside the coach, the passengers rode without talking. Betty snuggled close to her husband as Marshal Claxton and the bounty hunter eased back and dropped their hats low on their faces.

Larry Mangrum looked out the window, but periodically he swung his gaze to the face of the beautiful young woman across from him. Swaying with the movement of the stagecoach, Molly Wells seemed to be studying the rocks and patches of sagebrush that moved rapidly past her window, but from time to time, she would feel the pull of Larry's gaze, and when their eyes locked, her cheeks flushed slightly. Giving him a smile, she would once again look out the window.

After nearly an hour, Marshal Claxton stirred, lifted his hat from his face, and sat up straight. Rubbing his eyes, he looked around, relaxing again when he saw that his prisoner was still safely secured to the doorpost.

Betty Wells looked sharply at the marshal's face and said crustily, "Why does Pete have to be shackled to the post? Can't you see he is very uncomfortable?"

"I'm all right, honey," Wells said softly.

"Just because he wears a badge doesn't mean he has to be so callous," she said to Wells, eyeing Claxton disdainfully.

Claxton spoke in a gruff voice. "Your husband should have thought about his comforts before he took up robbing banks and stagecoaches, Mrs. Wells."

"I don't excuse what Pete did, Marshal," Betty said evenly, "but he didn't become an outlaw for greed or meanness like most of the others do. He tried to find honest work, and there just wasn't any. He was only providing for his family."

"By robbing other people's families," said Claxton tartly.

Betty had no rejoinder, and Wells said softly to her, "There's no sense arguing it with the marshal, honey. I did wrong, and I've got to pay for it. As far as he is concerned, I'm a dangerous criminal. He has to take due precaution."

"But he saw what you did back there with that mad bull!" Betty argued.

"Doing some good deeds don't make up for having done bad ones, Mrs. Wells," growled Claxton.

Betty had no more to say for the moment. She did a quick examination of Pete's wrists to see if they were chafing. Satisfied they were all right, she settled back in the seat.

Jack Parris was now awake, but he remained immobile, with his hat over his eyes. He was listening intently, thinking that John Claxton was in for a big surprise. Somewhere this side of Deadman Butte, Claxton would die.

When Parris had learned that an army platoon was to meet them at Deadman Butte, he realized he would have to make his move before they were in sight of it. He would do it a short while after they pulled out of Mayoworth, he had decided. He had also decided that the simplest way to handle it was to shoot everyone—crew and passengers—in one clean sweep. He would kill Pete Wells at the same time. Since the criminal was cuffed to the doorpost, he would pose no threat. The two women were not armed, so they would be easily disposed of. All Parris had to do was find the right time to gun down the marshal, the cowboy, the driver, and the shotgunner. He would get the drop on them by catching them off guard. The right moment would present itself. Of that he had no doubt.

Parris decided it was time to sit up, so he lifted his hat, yawned, and pushed it to the back of his head. Bumping the marshal and Larry Mangrum with his elbows, he stretched and yawned again. Claxton turned and set his probing eyes on Parris, almost as if the lawman were reading his mind.

Claxton unknowingly set butterflies flitting against the wall of Parris's stomach when he said, "Are you sure we haven't met somewhere before, Thompson?"

The bounty hunter looked at Claxton with an impassivity born of an iron will. "Sure as I am that my mother was a woman," he replied in a level tone.

The marshal then turned his attention to Larry Mangrum. As if he had been contemplating the subject, Claxton said, "Mangrum, you say you used to be a gunfighter?"

Larry Mangrum, wishing the lawman would stay off the subject of his past, said in a civil manner, "Yes, Marshal, I used to be. But I don't especially like to think about it."

"How does a man *quit* being a gunfighter?" Claxton pressed him. "Seems I'm always hearing that a man can't quit because if he lives very long as a gunfighter, it means he has to be plenty good. That being the case, there's always some young hopeful ready to brace him so's he can climb the ladder."

"Only thing a man can do is go where he's not known and start his life over," Larry said. He could feel Molly's eyes on him.

Claxton repositioned himself on the seat and said, "I heard you tell Miss Wells back at the stage office that you were going home to Rawlins on a permanent basis. I assume you came to Buffalo to make this new start in life."

"Yes, sir."

"How long you been in Buffalo?"

"Little over six months."

"Anybody recognize you and throw up a challenge since you've been here?"

"Only one, sir. And I was able to subdue him without shooting him."

Claxton rubbed his chin pensively, then asked, "How many men have you killed in gunfights?"

Larry uneasily pulled at his ear, purposely avoiding Molly's blue eyes. "Uh . . . five, sir. Five."

Claxton arched his eyebrows. "Five, huh? What were their names?"

Betty Wells was feeling a raw irritation at the marshal's prying into Larry's business, but she held her peace.

"Nobody you'd know, Marshal," said Larry.

"Try me," clipped Claxton.

Larry was chafing somewhat under the interrogation. He would not have minded it as much if the questioning had been done at another time and place, away from the present company. His cheeks took on a winter bleakness as he replied, "Billy Dearborn, Arlie Harris, Apache Jim Wyman, Chet Stone, and Duke Billings."

"I've heard of two of them," said Claxton. "Wyman and Stone. Those birds were supposed to be pretty fast."

"Yes, sir." Larry nodded, hoping the marshal would drop the subject.

However, it was not to happen quite yet. Claxton asked, "Any of these gunfights happen in Rawlins?"

"Yeah." Larry sighed. "The last one. Duke Billings."

"So you are known as a pretty fast man in your hometown."

"I guess you'd say so."

"Then why are you going back there on a permanent basis? Looks to me like you're wanting to get back in the gunfighting business. I mean, with going back where you're known as a gunfighter and wearing that iron tied down and all."

Larry Mangrum was nettled. It was none of John Claxton's business that he was returning to Rawlins to face Vic Spain and die. He certainly did not want the rest of the passengers to know about it. Especially Molly. Let her and the others find out about it when it was over. Sharpening his words slightly, he retorted, "That's my private business, Marshal Claxton. Since I'm not under arrest, I would rather not answer any more questions."

John Claxton hunched his thick shoulders and turned his attention out the window.

Good for you, Larry! thought Betty Wells, who had had her fill of the barrel-bellied lawman.

Up in the box Ross Blake and Hal Stacy were discussing the increasing threat of hostilities by the renegade Sioux. The virulent hatred for whites exhibited by Two Thumbs was spreading like a disease among other bands that had jumped the reservations. The Sioux nation had never been anything but an enemy to white men; they had killed the intruders who trespassed on their land for many years. But the vengeance of Two Thumbs seemed to have no respite whatsoever. His cunning and wicked mind had devised new and inhuman means of torture that could only be described as diabolical.

Letting his eyes constantly scan the surrounding territory, shotgunner Hal Stacy said, "Ross, how long do you think Two Thumbs will stay in Montana?"

"Till he kills enough whites in that area to satisfy his demonic mind," came Blake's reply. "Then he'll look for fresh meat elsewhere."

"Can't the army track him down and kill him?"

"They've been trying ever since he jumped the reservation over in Dakota nearly three years ago," responded Blake. "He's craftier than a fox. A lot of bluecoats have died trying to take him."

"I hope he stays out of Wyoming," Stacy said, raising his hat and sleeving sweat from his brow.

"Yeah," agreed Blake. "But I've got a feeling he's going to move north on us anytime now. Like you said this morning, I've been expecting him to attack our stages between Buffalo and Deadman Butte. We may have to have the army start escorting us the whole length of the trip."

Stacy shook his head, cast a glance at the lowering sun, and sleeved sweat again.

Inside the coach Marshal Claxton pulled his gaze from the window and picked up the rifle that lay at his feet. The rifles issued to Larry and Parris also lay flat on the floor.

As the marshal dropped the lever to expose the chamber, he said, "Haven't checked this since I pulled it from my saddleboot. Thought I'd best make sure it's loaded and working properly."

"There's a good chance we could get hit by Indians before we reach Deadman Butte, isn't there, Marshal?" asked Pete Wells.

"I'd say the possibility is a healthy one," answered the lawman, snapping the lever in place. "I don't trust those dirty devils as far as I could throw the Butte itself."

Wells said hesitantly, "Marshal, if Indians come at us, we're going to need all the firepower we can muster. I'm asking you as one human being to another, will you take off these cuffs and let me have a gun? I can get one from the crate in the rack."

Claxton looked at the man as if he had just seen him for the first time. "You must be kidding!" he blustered. "What kind of fool do you take me for? First chance you got, you'd plug me so you could escape."

"You know my record," Wells countered. "In all the robberies I pulled, I never shot anyone."

"You put a gun on 'em," Claxton replied icily.

"Yes, and I was wrong to do it, but I'm not a killer, Claxton. My wife and daughter are on this stage, and I'm concerned for their safety. I would like to help protect them should we run into hostiles."

"It isn't my fault these two women are on this stage, Wells," rasped Claxton. "I tried to talk 'em into going to Rawlins later, but they wouldn't listen. You're not getting out of the cuffs, much less getting your hands on a gun."

"Marshal," said Wells in an urgent tone, "the fact is, Betty and Molly *are* on the stage, and they must be protected. I'm asking you for their sake to let me have a rifle. I give you my word. I will only use the gun on attacking Indians."

Claxton threw his head back and laughed heartily, saying, "Since when is an outlaw's word any good?"

Betty's back stiffened, and a flush of color reddened her cheeks. "Marshal," she said sharply, "Pete realizes he made a big mistake in becoming an outlaw. Many a night he has lain awake with his guilt. But in the last two years he has totally changed. You saw what he did back there in town. How many outlaws would have done that? Pete has been an upstanding citizen in Buffalo. Certainly you detected that by the attitude of the people toward him. You heard J. D. Ryle leave him an open door for a job."

The lawman cleared his throat. "Mrs. Wells, I—"

"Ask Ross Blake!" cut in Betty. "He'll tell you—"

Her husband interrupted her by saying, "Honey, there's no use pushing the marshal any further."

"You're right about that," Claxton said flatly.

Wells said, "Would you at least give rifles to Betty and Molly, Marshal? They're both crack shots. I trained them myself. At least let them help in the fight if the Sioux come after us."

The federal man shook his head. "I can't believe what I'm hearing! I know P. T. Barnum said there's a sucker born every minute, but I'm not one of 'em! Do you think I've lived this long wearing a badge by giving guns to people who'll shoot me down the minute they get a chance? Hey, I'm not kidding myself. These two women don't want you locked up in prison for the next twenty years. If I give them guns, they'll turn them on me in order to free you. Now, I don't want to hear any more on the subject. The women are not getting guns!"

"Pardon me, Marshal," Larry Mangrum spoke up, "but Mrs. Wells and Miss Molly are not criminals. They have a right to defend themselves. Especially when we know what the Sioux do to white women."

Claxton swung his ponderous head around. His voice rang harshly as he snapped, "I said I don't want to hear any more on the subject, Mangrum! The women will get no guns! Now that's the end of the discussion!"

Up in the box, Hal Stacy turned to his boss and said,

"Sounds like a hot debate of some kind going on down there—like the marshal's sitting on a tack or something."

Ross Blake smiled. "Guess a little arguing helps to pass the time."

Stacy chuckled. "Maybe I ought to let Claxton come up here and cool off. I'd be glad to sit in that coach and feast my eyes on Miss Molly Wells."

"She *is* something to look at, I'll admit," replied Blake. "You ever try to court her?"

Stacy's ruddy face flooded with red. "Who, me?"

"There's nobody else sitting in this seat is there?"

"Aw shucks, Ross, a pretty thing like that would never be interested in the likes of me."

"Oh, I'm not so sure." Blake laughed, digging an elbow into the young man's ribs. "Opposites attract, you know!"

Stacy laughed, too, and then looking at the surrounding landmarks, he said, "Well, we're a good thirty miles out of Buffalo now. Won't be long till we get to Mayoworth. My legs can use a good str—"

The shotgunner's words were cut off as he straightened his back and squinted toward the south. "Ross . . ."

"Yeah?"

"Take a look at that bluff a little to the right about a mile away."

Ross Blake focused on a half-dozen mounted Sioux outlined against the sky on the tall bluff. "We've got trouble, Hal," he said in a serious tone. Leaning over the side and speaking toward his passengers inside the coach, he shouted, "Indians up ahead! Looks like only a few, but there may be more close by! Get ready!"

The Indians were now peeling off the bluff, shaking their feathered rifles in the air and barking like dogs.

Inside the coach, Claxton, Parris, and Larry Mangrum raised their rifles, pointing the muzzles out their respective windows. Pete Wells told his wife and daughter to get down on the floor, and then he said to Claxton, "If you'd let me have a gun, there would be two of us shooting out this window."

The marshal ignored him.

Blake's voice came again: "The bouncing of the coach will make it hard to be accurate, so shoot at their horses." Blake could be heard cracking a bullwhip over the team's heads, and then he shouted at the top of his lungs, "Here they come!"

The six horses lunged into the harness and went immediately into a full gallop, their manes and tails flying in the wind. The coach bounced and weaved across the bumpy land. Blake and Stacy watched as the six bronze-skinned warriors hit level ground and began making a wide circle off to their left. Stacy clutched his shotgun.

Inside the bounding vehicle, Marshal Claxton said to the others, "Blake's right. The horses will be a lot easier to hit than the Indians. Shoot for the pintos."

Larry and Jack Parris were shoulder-to-shoulder at the opposite window. Larry caught sight of the six riders and said, "They're coming at us from the east side."

"Let 'em get real close before you fire," Claxton told the other two men. "The closer the better. You can be more accurate that way."

Larry Mangrum looked down on the floor at Molly. Fear was written on her lovely face. He smiled and said, "It'll be all right, Miss Molly." She smiled back thinly.

The thundering hooves and spinning wheels were throwing up a huge cloud of dust as the stage sped on.

The Sioux were now swinging around so as to come at the rocking stage from behind. Their shouts could already be heard by those inside the coach.

Claxton leaned out his window, felt the wind pluck at his hat, and ducked back in. Removing the hat, he stuck his head back out, shouldering the rifle. Mangrum and Parris followed suit, removing their hats and bracing themselves for the attack.

The galloping Sioux split three and three to come up on

each side of the stage. They were strung out about thirty feet apart when the first two opened fire, their bullets chewing into the back wall of the coach.

"Don't fire yet!" yelled Claxton. "Let 'em get closer!"

Soon the Indians were close enough to reveal the red and blue spots of paint on their cheeks and the yellow stripes across their noses.

"Now!" shouted the marshal, and he fired. His bullet missed, and he heard one hum past his ear. He fired twice more as he heard Larry Mangrum and Jack Parris open up. Still Claxton's bullets found no mark.

Larry and the bounty hunter both learned quickly that a bouncing stage made a poor platform for accurate shooting. They also missed, firing two rounds each. The lead Indian on the coach's left side was pulling up close, and Larry let himself ride with the lurches of the stage as he squeezed off another shot, this one catching the pinto in the neck. It gave a death cry as blood spurted, and then it somersaulted, throwing its rider hard to the ground. The horse's body struck the Indian, crushing him violently. A warm sense of pleasure washed over the young cowboy as he observed it.

Betty Wells was on her knees close to her husband. With his hands shackled to the door post, he was especially vulnerable to the Indians' bullets and yet had no way to protect himself. Shouting at Claxton above the thunder of the rolling vehicle and the roar of the guns, Betty said, "The least you could do is release Pete and let him duck down, Marshal!"

Working the lever and firing, Claxton hollered back, "He stays where he is!"

Molly, her jaw squared, sat up straight and spoke loudly to the lawman, "My father would be a little safer if two guns were being fired from your window, Marshal!"

Claxton ignored her, but she thought that Larry Mangrum saw the sense of her statement. She observed it in his eyes as he gave her a quick glance, then turned back to the business at hand. "Larry!" she called. "Let me have your revolver!"

"Don't do it!" shouted Claxton without turning to look.

"No time to argue!" Larry called. "Here, Miss Molly, take my rifle!" As he handed Molly the rifle, he said to Parris, "Go shoot with the marshal! Let her stay here by me!"

Parris nodded and crawled to Claxton's side, shoving the muzzle of his rifle past Pete Wells's shackled hands. Claxton swore angrily at Larry, but he was too busy to do anything about it. Larry whipped out his revolver, eared back the hammer, and fired at the closest Indian's horse. His aim was spoiled by a sudden lurch of the coach, but Molly's first shot found its mark, and the pony went down headfirst. The Sioux astride it hit the ground hard, plowing dirt with his face.

Jack Parris shot a Sioux drawing near and sent him rolling on the ground. The remaining three Indians poured on the speed, firing wildly at the bouncing stage. The marshal hit a pinto in the chest, and horse and rider went down in a cloud of dust.

At the same time Hal Stacy, who had been waiting for the pursuing warriors to draw close enough to be within his shotgun's range, braced himself on the seat as one of the Sioux drew near. Aiming the twelve-gauge at the Indian's head, Stacy fired one barrel, but just as he squeezed the trigger, the coach hit a hard bump, throwing his aim off. The dark-skinned Sioux smiled wickedly and raised his rifle, lining it up to shoot Stacy.

Again the shotgunner took aim, this time pulling the second trigger. The big gun boomed, and the Indian's face disappeared in a mass of blood, his lifeless body hitting the ground and cartwheeling for several yards.

The remaining Indian drew rein, howling his frustration. In a final display of defiance, he released one last shot at the racing stage. Ross Blake kept the lathered horses at a full gallop for a long quarter of an hour, until the lone Indian was out of sight. Then he pulled to a stop. He could see Mayoworth in the distance.

Blake quickly climbed down from the box, followed by Hal Stacy. Pulling open the door, Blake asked breathlessly, "Is everybody all right?"

"Looks like we are," answered Larry Mangrum, stepping out of the vehicle.

Blake ran his gaze over the bullet-riddled coach and said, "That was some shooting! You all did real good!"

"Yeah," said Larry. "Even Molly. She bagged one with her first shot!"

As he climbed out of the stage, Marshal John Claxton growled, "You had no business giving her your gun, Mangrum! I told you not to do it! You disobeyed my explicit command!"

Color rushed swiftly to Molly's face, and her eyes flashed with glinting spirit. Bolting through the door, she handed Larry his rifle while looking at Claxton, and she said, "Here, Larry. I'm a dangerous outlaw. I might shoot Marshal Claxton!"

Anger flashed across the marshal's face. "I don't need your insolence, Miss Wells," he spat. "Your father is an outlaw, and I'm not taking any chances. No one is going to keep me from delivering him to the law at Rawlins."

Jack Parris, who had just stepped out of the stage, smiled smugly to himself.

Chapter Six

The sun was dipping behind the western horizon as the bullet-riddled coach pulled into Mayoworth. The town's business district was two blocks long, with houses and shacks scattered around it in a haphazard manner. Three saloons and the Buffalo Stage Line relay station were located on the corners of the town's only intersection.

People came from every direction as the coach rolled to a halt. There was a good deal of speculation that the coach had run into Indians. Charlie Kemper, a short, rotund man of sixty who was employed as Ross Blake's Mayoworth agent, bolted through the door of the station and approached Blake as he climbed down from the box.

"Ross," Kemper gasped, eyeing the stage, "did you meet up with the Sioux?"

As Blake's feet touched ground, he looked at Kemper. "Yeah, Charlie. Six of them hit us about five miles back."

"I'm not surprised," said the rotund man. "The dirty devils have been in the area. Massacred two ranch families west of here just yesterday."

"You don't suppose Two Thumbs has moved down here?" asked Blake.

"If he has, he wasn't in on yesterday's massacre," replied Kemper. "The ranch women were raped before they were killed, but no one was tortured. If there was no torture, there was no Two Thumbs."

Blake's dark head nodded in agreement.

By now Hal Stacy and the passengers had alighted, stretching their stiff bodies. The passengers were heading for the outhouses as Hal Stacy gave the fascinated towns-people a detailed account of the Indian attack. Blake helped Kemper hitch up a fresh team, while Bertha Kemper, Charlie's wife, cooked up a meal for the crew and passengers.

Dusk settled slowly across the land, purpling the Big-horn Mountains to the west and staining the broad sky with a deep, murky curtain. As Ross Blake sat down at the long table in the station with Hal Stacy and the passen-gers, he said, "No need to gulp down your food, folks. We have to move much slower at night, but we'll still arrive at the Deadman Butte station an hour or so after sunrise. The cavalry platoon won't begin to worry about us until eight o'clock."

Conversation at the table centered on the Sioux attack they had just experienced. Though Molly Wells sat next to her mother, while young Larry Mangrum was farther down the table, Molly periodically looked at him and found his eyes on her. Each time, she blushed, giving him a warm smile.

They were almost finished eating when loud, excited voices came from the street. Charlie Kemper hurried out the door, followed by Blake and Stacy. Within moments the others had filed out behind them.

Mayoworth's main street was well lighted with lanterns on tall poles. Light also streamed from the windows of the three saloons as bar patrons emptied out onto the street to see what was going on. People were crowding around a wagon that had pulled into town along with a half dozen men on horseback. In the bed of the wagon were several forms covered with gunnysacks and a small tarpaulin. The seat and sideboards of the wagon were smeared with what appeared to be blood.

The man in the wagon seat, who seemed to be leading the group of riders, told the people his name was Clete Spencer. He and his friends had been on their way north to Montana that morning when they had come upon the occupants of the wagon twenty-five miles north of Deadman Butte. The unfortunate victims had been brutally tortured before their throats had been slit.

When one of Mayoworth's male citizens stepped up to the wagon bed and began to remove the gunnysacks, Clete Spencer twisted around on the seat and said, "Don't do it, mister. You don't want to see it!"

But the wagon driver's warning was too late. The man got one full glimpse of the carnage and gagged.

After that Ross Blake moved up to the wagon and introduced himself to Clete Spencer, explaining that he was owner of the Buffalo Stage Line. "I'm driving the run to Rawlins," he said, "and I want to check out what happened to these folks. This torture you speak of makes me think Two Thumbs might be in the neighborhood."

As Blake stepped to the bed, raised the tarpaulin, and threw aside the gunnysacks, Larry Mangrum moved up beside him. The younger man gasped as he beheld the bodies—with noses missing, eyeballs gouged out, ears severed, and fingers and toes chopped off. Each throat had been cut from jawbone to jawbone.

Marshal John Claxton turned to Pete Wells, who stood beside him on the porch of the station, and said, "You stay put." With that, the bald lawman drew up beside Ross Blake and viewed the horrid scene. As Blake covered the bodies, Claxton said, "You think it was Two Thumbs?"

Turning away from the wagon, Blake noticed that all the color had drained from Larry Mangrum's face. To Claxton, he answered, "If it wasn't Two Thumbs, he's got somebody horning in on his kind of work."

Bounty hunter Jack Parris, posing as Ray Thompson,

scowled at the delay the wagonful of bodies was causing. The moon was rising, and he wanted to get going. He was eager to murder the occupants of the stage and take Pete Wells's body on to Rawlins for the reward. His plan was to stop the stage out on the prairie by feigning sickness. When he stepped out of the vehicle, he would take them all by surprise and gun them down.

Joining the three men at the wagon, he asked Blake, "Are we gonna go on?"

Ross Blake lifted his hat and ran his fingers through his brown hair. Shaking his head, he said, "Not tonight. Two Thumbs and his cutthroats have no qualms about attacking at night. Whatever you've heard about Indians not fighting at night because of their religion, you can forget it with Two Thumbs. One thing he's not is religious."

"That doesn't make sense to me," the bounty hunter said dryly.

"What do you mean?" queried Blake.

"If they come at us in the dark, we can see as good as they can. What difference does it make whether we fight them in daylight or dark?"

"A lot of difference," replied Blake. "It's not as easy to catch us with a sneak attack in the daylight. We're not going on until morning. Maybe when we don't show up at Deadman Butte by eight o'clock, the cavalry will come looking for us. Right now, I would welcome their presence."

The bounty hunter knew he might arouse Blake's suspicions if he argued, so he dropped it. He would carry out his plan the next day.

Marshal Claxton wheeled slowly, intending to move back to his prisoner. Suddenly one of the riders with Clete Spencer set his eyes on the bounty hunter and exclaimed, "Hey, Parris! Jack Parris, you ol' saddletramp! I just recognized you!" Sliding from his horse's back, he said, "When did you start dressin' fancy like that and wearin' your hair like a decent citizen?"

Parris's backbone tingled as he saw the marshal halt in

his tracks and whip his head around. Claxton was apparently aware of the name of the infamous bounty hunter.

Jack Parris felt his heart grow cold as the rider approached him with his right hand extended. "Hey, ol' pard, don't you remember me? Dolph Williams. From Scottsbluff."

The bounty hunter turned to face Williams but did not offer his hand. He could feel the hot eyes of the marshal on the back of his head as Claxton stomped toward him, grabbed Parris's shoulder, and spun him around.

Anger flashed in Claxton's eyes as he said. "Now I know why you looked familiar, you lying snake! You and I met in Rock Springs three or four years ago. You're a scaly-bellied bounty hunter!"

Pete Wells got the picture immediately. From the side of his mouth he said to his wife and daughter, "I know of this guy, too. He's after *me*."

Betty's hand went to her mouth as Molly squeezed her father's arm and bit down on her lower lip.

Jack Parris took a step back, feeling the pressure of the marshal's wrath. "Now, look, Claxton," he said, forcing his voice to remain calm. "I was just—"

"Don't try to snow me!" blustered the marshal. "You got on that stage posing as a businessman! You're lying for a reason, and I know what that reason is—Pete Wells."

Parris shook his head vigorously. "You got it all wrong, Claxton. I'm trying to turn over a new leaf and make my living another way!"

The angry marshal closed the gap between them, moving so close that his nose was only an inch from the bounty hunter's. "Yeah? Like what?"

Jack Parris's mind was numb. This whole thing had come on too quickly, and he could not think of anything believable. His tongue seemed stuck to the roof of his mouth.

Seeing the man's dilemma, Claxton asked pointedly, "If

I'm wrong about you being after Wells, tell me why you're on this trip to Rawlins."

"Private business," Parris said levelly, trying to put up a smoke screen. "I can't reveal it."

Claxton looked at him with obvious disbelief. His lips pulled tight as he rasped, "Your trip ends right here, Parris. You won't be riding the stage any farther."

The bounty hunter could feel the five thousand dollars slipping away from him, but his greed refused to let go. His voice grew wild as he blinked and said, "You can't do that, Claxton! I paid my fare all the way to Rawlins. I have every right to ride that stage!"

When the marshal countered, saying Parris could take the next one, the bounty hunter argued back that his private business demanded that he be in Rawlins sooner than that. Claxton smirked, saying life had some tough breaks.

As the lawman and the bounty hunter continued to argue, three rough-looking men stood on the porch of one of the saloons. The tallest of the men turned to the other two and said, "Does the name Jack Parris ring a bell with you boys?"

"Yeah, Giff," one of the men replied. "He's the bounty hunter who sent Max to prison."

The third man chuckled. "I bet Max would be happier than a chicken hawk with a fat pullet if we brought Parris to him."

"That's what I was thinkin'," said the man named Giff. "Max might get so happy he'd take us into his new gang when he leaves the Hole-in-the-Wall."

At that moment, a dirty, unshaven man with his gun slung low materialized out of the shadows from across the street. He moved in a straight line for the three outlaws. As the unshaven man approached the trio, the second man on the porch spotted him and said with a grin, "Hey, Clyde, lookee who's here!"

The third man's face broke into a smile as he recognized

the newcomer. "Well, Earl, I'll be a suck-egg mule! If it ain't Blackie!"

"Earl Smith and Clyde Zimmerman!" the man named Blackie exclaimed as he shook hands with his two friends and they slapped him on the back. "You boys look just as ugly as I remembered!" He glanced over at the tall man. "How about introducing me to your friend."

Earl Smith turned to his partner and said, "Giff, this is Blackie Doss. You've heard us talk about him." Lowering his voice and looking around, he added, "Blackie was with us down in New Mexico on that Santa Fe bank job."

"Oh, sure." The tall man grinned, extending his hand. "I'm Giff Mudd, Blackie."

"Where you from?" inquired Doss.

"Just a minute," said Smith, raising a palm and looking toward the center of the street. "We gotta hear the end of this argument."

By now Ross Blake had entered the heated conversation between Claxton and Parris. "Marshal," he was saying, "I'll refund Mr. Parris's money and let him sleep here in the station until the next stage comes through. He can ride it free all the way to Rawlins."

"Thank you." Claxton nodded, and then looking at Parris, he said, "You can't ask for a better deal than that, Jack. Your important private business will just have to wait."

Jack Parris was totally flustered. He knew he had to stay on the stage in order to end up with the reward money. "Look, Marshal," he said, keeping his tone sweet, "I'm sorry I've been argumentative, but my new career depends on my meeting a certain man in Rawlins within the next two days. There's no way I can prove it to you, but it's the truth. I'm sworn to secrecy. Believe me, there's nothing underhanded about it, but it's a business situation that I can't tell you or anyone else about."

Claxton looked at Blake. "What do you think?"

Blake shrugged his wide shoulders. "I guess he could be

telling you the truth. You really don't have a legal reason for putting him off the stage. He lied about his identity, but he hasn't broken any laws."

Looking at Parris with suspicion, Claxton said stiffly, "You can ride the stage on one condition, Parris—you must be unarmed and in handcuffs."

The bounty hunter flinched as though stung with a hot iron. "Unarmed?" he echoed. "In handcuffs! After what we went through today? And what we've seen here tonight? There's no way—"

"Fine," clipped the marshal, turning away. "You can wait for the next stage then."

Parris thought it over quickly. Even shackled and unarmed, he might still find a way to get hold of a gun and carry out his plan. If he was not on the stage, all hope of laying hands on the five thousand dollars would be gone. "Okay, okay," he called after Claxton. "I'll go along with you. But I must be in Rawlins day after tomorrow."

"Fine," said the marshal. "So be it."

The four men standing on the saloon porch had heard the end of the dispute involving the bounty hunter. When the outcome was clear, Earl Smith said to Clyde Zimmerman and Giff Mudd, "Okay, boys. Parris is gonna be on the stage in the mornin'. Let's go back inside and have a drink with Blackie."

As the outlaws settled at a table in the saloon, Blackie Doss asked, "What's this all about, fellas?"

Pouring drinks all around from a full bottle, Smith said to Mudd, "You have any objections if I tell him, Giff?"

"Won't bother me," replied Mudd.

Smith set his eyes on Doss and said, "Well, Blackie, it's like this. We've been hidin' out at the Hole-in-the-Wall for about three months now, kinda lettin' things cool off. Clyde and I pulled a bank job over in Cheyenne back in March. We were feelin' a little closed in, so we ventured out today for the first time. Giff here showed up at the

Hole about the same time we did. He's on the dodge, too."

"I've never been to the Hole-in-the-Wall," said Doss. "Exactly where is it?"

"Twenty-three miles due south of here," responded Smith.

Doss nodded. "So what's the deal on this guy Parris?"

"He's a stinkin' bounty hunter," said Zimmerman. "We got a pal out in the Hole named Max Lund. Max escaped prison down in Canon City, Colorado, in April, and now he's hidin' at the Hole. All we've heard since he got there is how much Max hates Jack Parris. It was Parris who captured him and turned him in at Denver for a thousand dollars reward money."

"Yeah," put in Smith. "Max has been livin' for the day he felt it was safe to leave the Hole and go huntin' for Parris. He wants to kill him so bad he can taste it."

"Max is gonna start up a new gang," added Zimmerman, "and we want to get in on it. So we figure if we take Parris to him, that would just about cinch up our gettin' into his new gang."

"Thing for us to do, boys," said Earl Smith, "is follow the stage and waylay it where nobody can give us any trouble. We'll take Parris off the stage and hightail it for the Hole."

"Sounds good to me," said Giff Mudd. "Let's drink to it."

By eight o'clock that evening, Mayoworth's excitement had settled down, and the street was back to normal. The discordant sound of three pianos coming from the saloons filled the night air. The crew and passengers of Ross Blake's stagecoach were seated in the way station. With a cautious eye on Pete Wells, Marshal Claxton carried on a conversation with Blake and Stacy, while Jack Parris sat in a corner alone, pondering his situation.

Pete and Betty Wells sat together, talking in low tones. Seated across from each other at the dining table, Molly Wells and Larry Mangrum were discussing the Indian danger. After some time, Molly said, "Larry, it's stuffy in here. Would you like to go out and get some fresh air?"

"Sure, Miss Molly," replied the lanky cowboy, rising to his feet.

Molly moved to where her parents sat and told them she and Larry were going for a walk. They would be back shortly.

The night air was cool as the pair walked southward down the street. Within moments they were at the edge of town and beyond the light of the streetlamps. The three-quarter moon floated like a silver disc in the star-studded sky, shedding its soft light over the rugged land. As they walked slowly, Molly said, "Larry, it was more than fresh air I wanted by taking this walk."

"What do you mean, Miss Molly?"

"Well, you can tell me it's none of my business if you want to, but I sense there is something troubling you about your return to Rawlins. I thought maybe it would help you to talk about it."

Larry's muscles tightened. He was not aware that his dread of facing Vic Spain had been that obvious. But he could not reveal his purpose for returning to Rawlins. If he did, he was afraid that Molly would lose what respect she now had for him. He was about to say that it was a deeply personal thing and he would rather not talk about it when she shook his defenses by asking a blunt question.

"Has your return home got anything to do with that tied-down gun on your hip?"

Larry's feet seemed to turn to stone. He stopped and looked down at her searching eyes in the moonlight. "Why do you ask that?" he queried, puzzled as to what to tell her.

Molly lifted her graceful shoulders and then let them down quickly. "Just a feeling I have."

Towering over her, he was awed by her captivating beauty, enhanced by the silver light from the sky. His mind was spinning. In an attempt to avoid the subject of the pending gunfight, he found himself saying, "Miss Molly, you are the most beautiful woman I have ever seen in my life."

Molly's face reddened. Dropping her eyes momentarily, she said, "I—I appreciate your kindness, Larry."

"It's not kindness," he said softly. "It's the truth."

Lifting her gaze back to his, she said, "I am flattered by what you say. But you didn't answer my question."

Larry could not bring himself to lie to this lovely woman; the truth had to come out. Sighing deeply, he said, "I didn't want to tell you because I don't want you to think poorly of me. But I won't lie to you, Miss Molly. I am going back to Rawlins to face a gunfighter named Vic Spain."

"Vic Spain!" she exclaimed. "But Larry, he's one of the best! I'm sure you are good, but the man has many years of experience. I've heard about him since I was eight or nine years old. He killed many of the top gunfighters in the West. Why would you go up against him?"

"Well, it's not your average situation, Miss Molly," Larry replied. "It's a long story."

"I'd like to hear it," she said.

"All right. I'll make it as short as possible."

The tall, curly-headed cowboy then proceeded to tell Molly the story behind his return home to face the dangerous Vic Spain. When he had finished, they were headed back toward town, but still a half mile from its edge. Molly gripped one of Larry's hands and looked up at him with deep concern in her eyes. "Larry, you must not go through with this! Certainly there is something the law can do about Spain. Can't the marshal there do something to protect your parents from him?"

"It isn't just my parents who are in danger, Miss Molly," said Mangrum. "Spain's threat sounded broad enough that he might hurt someone else in Rawlins if I don't show up."

She took hold of his other hand, squeezing hard. "But you can't just go into this thing knowing you're going to die!"

Mangrum was thrilled at her touch and at the concern she was showing for his life, but he said, "Miss Molly, I can't let someone else suffer harm in order to save myself. I could report Spain's threat to the marshal, but it's not enough to jail him on. And the marshal can't watch him all the time. Besides, I've shamed my parents enough by gunfighting and drinking in the first place. If I don't face Spain, I'll be known as a coward. It's all over town that he has come to Rawlins for a showdown with me. Even if he didn't hurt my parents, I can't make them live with the shame that their son is a coward. I don't have a choice, Miss Molly. I'm on a one-way track, and there's no turning back."

The beautiful young woman slipped her arm inside Larry's as they neared the town's edge. "There has to be some way out of this," she said solemnly. "There just has to be."

A tremor ran through Larry's body as Molly clung to his arm. He wished things were different. If he were free to do it, he could let himself fall in love with Molly Wells so easily. Taking a deep breath and letting it out slowly, he said, "But there isn't. There is no way out."

After a sleepless night, Molly Wells climbed aboard the stage at sunrise with a cold, hollow feeling in her heart. She was having strong feelings toward Larry Mangrum, and she did not want him to die.

Pete Wells was being cuffed to the same doorpost as before when Betty climbed in and took her place between him and Molly. Larry stepped in and took his original seat across from the lovely blonde. Her smile warmed his heart, but there was sadness evident in her eyes.

Blake and Stacy were checking the harness with Charlie Kemper as Marshal Claxton rounded the coach after shackling his prisoner to the doorpost. The marshal was waiting for Jack Parris to come out of the station. Claxton had procured a second set of handcuffs from his small suitcase in the boot, and they dangled from his hand as Parris appeared in the doorway. The bounty hunter's face went sour when he saw the marshal waiting. Without a word, he walked to where Claxton stood and extended his wrists, placing them together. The movement rustled his suitcoat, exposing the empty holster on his waist.

Claxton said, "Not that way, Parris. Turn around."

The bounty hunter's brow furrowed. "Turn around? Aw, come on, Claxton! I can't ride in there with my hands cuffed behind my back!"

"You agreed to ride cuffed, pal," snarled Claxton.

Parris showed a flare of anger. "You didn't say it had to be with my hands behind me!"

"I don't recall saying it would be with your hands in front of you, either!" growled the lawman. "Do what I say or wait for the next stage."

Parris swore and turned around, placing his wrists together behind his back, and Claxton snapped the cuffs on, the ratchets making a hollow, clicking sound. When the bounty hunter entered the coach and sat down, he was still swearing under his breath. The marshal stepped into the coach, squeezed onto the seat beside Parris, and closed the door.

Blake and Stacy were now climbing up to the box. "Everybody in?" called Blake as he reached the high seat.

"They are," volunteered Charlie Kemper from beside the coach.

The stagecoach rocked and swayed on the uneven ground as the brilliant sun inched its way up from the eastern horizon. The two men on top watched for Indians, while inside the coach Betty Wells turned to her daughter and said, "Molly, you seem withdrawn this morning. Is there something bothering you? I mean, besides what we've had to face of late?"

Molly looked at Larry. He had not told her to keep the situation a secret, but she would not tell it until he said it was all right. Forcing a smile, she answered, "I'm okay, Mother. Guess I didn't sleep very well."

"That's understandable, honey," said Betty, satisfied with her daughter's answer.

A half hour had passed when the stage dipped into a long, deep draw. The tilting of the vehicle caused those facing forward to brace themselves in order to stay in their seats. Jack Parris made a big thing of it, complaining that his position was very uncomfortable, and the marshal reminded him that it was much more comfortable back at the relay station. Parris said no more but renewed his vow that Claxton was going to die a horrible death.

As the stage slowed and climbed out of the draw, it passed between two giant boulders, both of which were three feet taller than the top of the coach. "Have your shotgun ready as we pull out of here, Hal," Blake said to the shotgunner. "It would be a good place for redskins to try to take us."

Stacy cocked both hammers of his twelve-gauge and poised himself, eyes darting from side to side.

They were almost to the end of the boulders when a tall figure scurried over the rocky surface, leaped, and landed on the trunks in the rack. As both men turned to see the source of the sound, they were looking into the black, ominous muzzle of a Colt .45.

"Faces forward!" barked Giff Mudd. "No funny stuff, or you're dead! Just pull the stage past these rocks and put on the brake!"

Chapter Seven

Ross Blake pulled the stagecoach to a halt as soon as it had cleared the boulders. Inside the stage, John Claxton, who had heard the thump on top of the stage and the outlaw's harsh threat, started to open the door next to him when a mean-looking man appeared, thrusting a revolver in his face. "Stay right where you are, Marshal!" the man snapped.

"What's the meaning of this?" demanded Claxton. "There's no money on this stage!"

At the same instant, a third outlaw appeared on the other side. As Larry Mangrum's hand dropped to the butt of his Colt .45, the mean-looking man barked, "I want everybody's hands where I can see 'em! Now!"

The two women lifted their hands so they could be seen through the windows, as did Claxton and Larry Mangrum. The third outlaw, Clyde Zimmerman, took note of Pete Wells's wrists cuffed to the doorpost. Setting his gaze inside the coach at Jack Parris, he shouted angrily, "You, too, Parris! Get your hands where I can see 'em!"

"I can't!" retorted the bounty hunter. "They're cuffed behind my back!" Parris swung his head both ways, scrutinizing the faces of the outlaws. Neither was familiar. How did they know his name?

"Good!" exclaimed Zimmerman. "That'll make it all the easier."

"What are you talking about?" Claxton asked tartly.

"We ain't after no money, Marshal," the mean-looking man, Earl Smith, said from where he stood brandishing his gun. "All we want is Jack Parris."

"Now wait a minute!" snapped Claxton. "You have no business—"

"Shut up!" clipped Smith. "We ain't takin' no lip from nobody! Understand? And we ain't in no mood for somebody actin' a hero. We got a man on top of the stage holdin' a gun on your driver and his pal. One false move by any of you inside and those two on top die!"

Claxton eased back on the seat and sighed.

On top of the coach, Giff Mudd said to Hal Stacy, "Ease down the hammers on the shotgun, mister."

As Stacy obeyed, Mudd said, "Throw it on the ground." When the shotgun clattered on the hard earth, he added, "Now do the same with the iron on your hip."

Stacy reluctantly tossed his pistol to the ground.

Addressing the owner of the Buffalo Stage Line, Mudd said, "Okay, driver, you're next. That rifle by your feet— throw it down, and follow it with your revolver."

Before the stage had pulled out, the marshal had given Jack Parris's revolver to Ross Blake, and the driver had laid it on the floor of the box near his left foot. Now, carefully covering the gun with his foot, he tossed his own revolver and his rifle to the ground.

"Okay, boys!" called Mudd. "The cat's claws are pulled up here."

Holding his weapon steady on the marshal, Clyde Zimmerman blustered, "All right, lawman, let's have your sidearm. I know you'll have a rifle, too, so let's have it."

When the marshal was disarmed, Earl Smith did the same to Larry Mangrum, also taking Larry's rifle and the one Jack Parris had used.

"Okay," said Zimmerman, "everybody out!"

As the passengers, minus Pete Wells, came out one by one with their hands in the air, Jack Parris looked at the outlaws and said, "What do you want with me? How do you know my name?"

Before Zimmerman could answer, John Claxton growled, "I'm a United States marshal! You men are treading on federal ground throwing your guns on me. You had best back off. Just get on your horses and ride, or you'll suffer the consequences."

"You be a good boy, Marshal, and we won't touch you," Giff Mudd said from where he stood on the two trunks. "Like my pal said, all we want is this scaly bounty hunter."

Turning to look up at Mudd, Parris asked, "Why do you want me? I've never seen any of you before."

Ignoring Parris, Mudd looked at the lawman and said, "I see you've got Mr. Parris in cuffs, Marshal. What's he done?"

"None of your business," Claxton said tightly.

Mudd grinned. "No matter. He's ours now, anyway."

Earl Smith rounded the coach to where the passengers were assembled. He stepped up to Parris and flipped his coat back, exposing the empty holster. Looking at Claxton, he said, "Where's his gun?"

"In the rear boot," lied the marshal with a toss of his head.

Anger began to have its way with Jack Parris, swamping his sense of caution. Running his flinty gaze among the outlaws, he blared, "I asked you what you want with me! I don't know any of you!"

Still holding his gun on Blake and Stacy, Mudd looked down at Parris from the roof of the coach and said, "We want you for a pal of ours, bounty hunter. You turned him in for a pocketful of money."

"Who're you talking about?" demanded Parris, appearing to be unafraid.

"Max Lund!" came the quick reply.

The bounty hunter's face lost a little color at the mention of Max Lund, the thin shell of his bravado showing signs of cracking. "You been in prison with him?" he asked, his throat constricting.

"Nope. Max ain't in prison. He escaped. He's hidin' out at the Hole-in-the-Wall, and is he ever gonna be happy to see you. He's been sayin' how much he'd like to kill you an inch at a time. Looks like he's gonna get his wish!"

Parris, his features now ashen, looked at Claxton. With a whiny voice he said, "Marshal, you gotta protect me! You can't let them take me!"

One of the horses in the team blew, throwing its weight slightly into the harness, and the movement caused the stage to lurch a little. Ross Blake reached down and gripped the reins, tightening them, and as he did he felt the lump of the revolver under his left foot. He thought about trying to take out the three outlaws but knew his chances were slim. The life of the bounty hunter was not worth it.

John Claxton looked blandly at Jack Parris and said, "If I turn you over to these men, it will solve my problems with you."

"I won't cause you any problem!" Parris half screamed. "Just don't let them take me! Max Lund will kill me!"

"A lot the marshal can do about it," spoke up Earl Smith, now standing inches from Clyde Zimmerman. "We've got his gun."

Claxton set cold eyes on Zimmerman and Smith and then swung them to Mudd. In a steady voice he said, "I'm still giving you three a chance to change your minds about this. You mess with a federal man and you're in real trouble. Get on your horses and ride . . . without Parris."

Mudd laughed hoarsely. "Hey, boys, listen to the big man talk! He acts like *he's* holdin' a gun on *us!*"

Zimmerman and Smith laughed heartily, and then Smith said with a snarl, "Listen lawman! There's nothin' to stop us from killin' you and the rest of these birds. With all of you dead, we can take Parris to our pal at the Hole, and there won't be a peep out of you." Turning his wicked eyes on the two blond women, he added with a leer, "We'll take these lucious ladies with us, too."

"Hey, Earl," Mudd called from his high perch. "You're talkin' my language now!"

From where he sat in the coach, Pete Wells stiffened and blared, "No, you don't, you dirty scum! You're not taking my wife and daughter anywhere!"

At the thought of the outlaws' dirty hands on Molly, Larry Mangrum felt his blood heat up. With venom in his voice, he said, "Not a one of you is going to touch those women!"

Smith pointed a stiff finger at the cowboy. Eyes bulging, he hissed, "You shut up, mister! My vote is that you die first!" Looking at Giff Mudd, he said, "How about it, Giff?"

Realizing that all of their lives were now threatened, Ross Blake knew he had no choice. There was a gun within reach, and he was going to have to use it. His hands were still holding the reins tight, and he had never set the brake as Mudd had told him to do. As Mudd opened his mouth and told Smith to go ahead and shoot Larry, Blake snapped the reins and reached for the revolver in one quick move.

The horses reacted by leaping into the harness, causing the stage to lurch forward. Giff Mudd, taken by surprise, lost his footing and fell backward from the top of the coach, bouncing hard as he struck the edge of the rack and tumbled over the side. His gun flew from his hand and hit the ground before he did. Larry Mangrum dived for the weapon as the stunned outlaw was rolling to his knees.

At the same instant that Blake picked up the gun at his feet, he tightened the reins, halting the horses. He quickly brought the gun to bear on Clyde Zimmerman and fired. Zimmerman, shot in the shoulder, spun around and fell, the gun flying from his hand. Blake turned to see Earl Smith swinging his gun toward him, and the ex-cavalry officer shot him between the eyes. Smith's weapon fired harmlessly into the air as the impact of the slug snapped his head back, sending his body reeling to flop like a rag doll to the ground.

The others watched as Larry Mangrum seized Mudd's revolver and turned to meet the outlaw. Mudd had dipped his fingers behind his belt where he carried a small derringer, which was now visible to the cowboy. Larry shouted, "Don't do it!"

But Mudd did not heed the warning. As the small weapon came out ready for action, Larry fired, hitting the outlaw in the chest. Mudd collapsed, breathed out a vile oath, and died.

In the midst of the shooting, Clyde Zimmerman had staggered to his horse and made his way into the saddle. As the sound of the last shot died out and the smoke began to clear, everyone heard Zimmerman's horse galloping away. Larry Mangrum fired several shots after him, but he was already out of pistol range. Turning to Blake, who was dropping off the box, Mangrum said, "I'll take one of these horses and go after him."

"Let him go," Blake said, eyeing the two dead outlaws. "We need to stay on the move."

Molly Wells dashed to Larry and said breathlessly, "Oh, Larry, you were marvelous! That was a brave thing to do!"

The lanky young man dipped his chin slightly. "It was no more than any other man would do, Miss Molly," he said humbly. "I wasn't going to let those dirty skunks take you and your mother with them."

Molly's eyes danced with admiration for the handsome cowboy. She thought of his date with death in Rawlins, and a wave of sadness washed over her. Laying a hand gently on his arm, she said softly, "It means a lot to me that you cared."

Their glances came tenderly together, and for a wordless moment they looked deep into each other's eyes. When the spell was broken by Ross Blake's voice saying they needed to get going, they both knew they shared special feelings for each other.

Leaving the dead outlaws for the buzzards, Ross Blake drove the stage onward. Jack Parris was still cuffed with his hands behind his back, and Pete Wells was shackled as usual to the doorpost. The sun climbed higher in the sky, the temperature steadily rising.

As the stagecoach rocked along, Larry Mangrum noticed Jack Parris staring at Molly. He gave the bounty hunter a hard look, but Parris only smiled at him.

Unaware of what was going on between the two men, Molly was gazing out her window. She knew in her heart that she was falling in love with the handsome young man, and she was determined to find a way to keep Larry from facing the famous gunfighter. It was so foolish for him to die when he had his whole life before him. *Especially if we could spend it together*, she thought.

As Molly pulled her gaze back inside the coach, she found Jack Parris looking at her with hungry eyes. Flashing him a cold look of contempt, she turned her attention to Larry Mangrum, who smiled at her. As Molly looked across the coach at him, it was as if she were reading his thoughts. The pathos of his situation stirred her sensitive nature, and before she could stop herself, she blurted out, "Larry, you musn't do it. You mustn't! There has to be a way out!"

All eyes turned to the disconcerted young woman. Pete Wells, obviously troubled by her outburst, asked, "What are you talking about, Molly?"

Tears glistened in Molly's eyes. "Larry's going home to get himself killed, Daddy. He's going to face Vic Spain in a gunfight!"

"Vic Spain!" bellowed John Claxton.

Jack Parris's eyes widened.

"*The* Vic Spain?" asked Pete Wells, looking at Mangrum.

"Yes," Larry answered quietly, his features stolid.

Molly knuckled a tear from her left cheek. "I'm sorry,

Larry," she apologized. "I know you didn't mean for it to become public knowledge."

The dark-haired young man afforded her a warm smile. "It's all right, Miss Molly," he said in a tender tone. "I really don't mind who knows about it." It was true, Larry thought; the only regret he had about the others knowing of his pending gunfight was that there were now more people who would attempt to persuade him to give it up.

Betty set her kind gaze on Larry Mangrum and said, "Why are you doing this, Larry?"

"Yeah," grunted Claxton. "You told me your gunfighting days were over."

Sighing deeply, Larry said, "It isn't what it appears to be, Marshal. I know I don't have a chance against Spain." Running his gaze over the faces of his fellow passengers, he sighed again. "Let me tell you the story."

While the stage rocked and bounced across the sun-baked land and the humming wheels stirred up dust, Larry told his story. He finished by saying, "So you see, there's no way out. If I don't face Spain in a shootout, my parents and other innocent people in Rawlins will be hurt."

John Claxton swung a meaty fist through the air and said, "I'll find some reason to get Spain locked up, kid. If you go up against him, it's suicide for sure."

Larry gave the marshal a dubious look. "I appreciate your concern, sir, but how long could you keep Spain locked up?"

Claxton hunched one shoulder, "Well, I, uh—"

"When he got out I would have it to do anyway, Marshal. So I might just as well get it over with as soon as possible."

Pete Wells spoke up. "Maybe if you stay away, Larry, the marshal might be able to work with the law in Rawlins and run Spain out of town."

Mangrum shook his head. "Even if he could, that wouldn't stop Spain from sneaking back and harming my parents or some other innocent people. He's determined to have vengeance for my killing his nephew."

The discussion went on with everyone entering in except Jack Parris, who was deep in thought. Every turn of the coach's wheels took them closer to Deadman Butte, and once they were there, in the presence of the cavalry platoon, his chances of overcoming Claxton and those on the stage would be gone. He had to find some way to get the cuffs off his wrists. With the delays the coach had experienced, the cavalry might already be coming this way in search of it. Parris had to make his play soon.

While the conversation went on, Parris found himself staring once again at the beautiful young blond woman. Molly happened to look at him at that moment, giving him an icy glare and looking away. But the incident did not escape the notice of Larry Mangrum. Larry's eyes reached the bounty hunter with a sullen, sallow flash of anger. It was then that Parris decided how he would try to get the cuffs removed from his wrists. Once it was done, he would have to play it by ear. But one way or another, he was going to get hold of a gun and wipe out the whole bunch of them.

It was midmorning when Ross Blake wheeled the stage to a stop beside a water hole. As he and Stacy stepped down, he said to his passengers, "Okay, everybody. Time to water the horses and ourselves. Keep your eyes peeled for Indians."

Hal Stacy took a bucket and began dipping water for the horses. The passengers filed from the stage, stretching their hot, tired limbs. Claxton released Pete Wells from the doorpost, hastily fastening the handcuffs to his wrists once more. Canteens were given to the ladies first, then passed among the men. The marshal held the canteen to Jack Parris's mouth so he could drink.

Ross Blake approached Mangrum and said, "Larry, I

picked up some of the conversation from the box. I know it's none of my business, but I'm going to say it anyhow. Don't throw your life away. You've got too much to live for. There are laws to protect people from men like Vic Spain. Let some of us go into Rawlins and tell the marshal there what's going on. He can appoint some men to work as bodyguards for your parents."

"Spain is too slick, Mr. Blake," argued the cowboy. "He'd get past the bodyguards. But even if he didn't, Spain would hurt somebody else to take out his spite. I can't let that happen. I have to go and finish this thing once and for all." He paused for a moment and then added, "Besides, I've put enough shame on my parents without making them live with the disgrace of having a coward for a son."

Blake studied the open, honest face of Larry Mangrum. "You've got guts," he said, clapping a hand on his shoulder. "But it just seems to me there must be some way out of this for you."

"I've studied every angle, Mr. Blake," Larry responded. "I don't know what it would be."

The broad-shouldered ex-cavalry officer turned and spoke to the group. "Two Thumbs may very well be in this area. What we saw back there in Mayoworth was just his brand of brutality. We're still about eleven or twelve hours from Deadman Butte, and I'm hoping the army will come looking for us since we're so late. The quicker we have their protection, the better. But until that time, we must all stay alert and keep our eyes open. I have a feeling that the Indians who lived through the attack yesterday will return to their camp and bring some of their pals to jump us again."

Pete Wells lifted his shackled wrists level with his face and said to Blake, "All the more reason these should come off so I can handle a gun."

"Forget it, Wells!" the marshal cut in. "Those cuffs aren't coming off until you're behind bars in Rawlins!"

"We may not reach Rawlins, Marshal!" Betty fired back at him. "If those Indians come at us before we meet up with the cavalry, you're going to wish you had a hundred men like Pete wielding guns!"

Claxton turned away in a huff.

Blake talked with Pete and Betty, telling them he would trust Pete with his life but explaining that he could not go against Claxton. As they talked, Larry Mangrum excused himself to Molly and went to see if he could be of help to Hal Stacy, who was still watering the horses.

Molly turned slowly, dabbed at the perspiration on her brow, and walked to the rear of the coach. She was scanning the land in search of any movement when she became aware that someone was standing behind her. Pivoting partially, she saw it was the bounty hunter. "What do you want?" she clipped.

A lecherous grin spread across Parris's craggy face. "You and me could be beautiful together, honey," he said. "Why don't we run off? Just the two of us."

A look of disgust etched itself on Molly's face. "I can't think of anything more repulsive," she said tartly.

Parris moved closer to her, his warm breath touching her face as he said, "Who do you think you're fooling? I've seen the way you look at me. You find me very attractive, don't you? How's about a little kiss?"

Molly stiffened. Curling a lip over her teeth, she hissed, "I'd rather kiss a sidewinder!"

"Oh, yeah?" As Parris spoke, he thrust his head forward and pressed his lips to Molly's. She backed away quickly, making a gagging sound as she unleashed an open-handed blow across his face. Parris was somewhat off balance when the slap stung his face, and with his hands cuffed behind his back, he stumbled, swearing at her.

Every head was turned in their direction now, and Pete Wells was on the run toward them. Larry Mangrum was rounding the coach at a fast clip. Molly made another gagging sound, spit in the dirt, and wiped the back of her hand across her mouth.

Pete Wells slammed Parris with the full weight of his body. The two men hit the ground, and Wells was on top of the bounty hunter immediately, pounding his face savagely though his wrists were shackled together in front of him.

Larry drew up to Molly, asking, "What did he do?"

Spitting and wiping her mouth again, she said, "He put his dirty lips on mine!"

"I'm sorry, Miss Molly," he said, patting her arm. "I promise you. He'll never do it again!"

With that, the cowboy whirled and headed toward the scuffling pair. Parris was nearly helpless with his hands cuffed behind his back, but he was attempting to get in a position to kick his assailant anywhere possible. At that moment Marshal Claxton drew up and pulled Wells off the bounty hunter. "That's enough, boys," he said.

"He forced himself on my daughter!" rasped Wells, breathing hotly and jerking his arms loose from Claxton's grip. "I'm gonna teach him a lesson!"

Rising to his feet, the bounty hunter jutted his jaw and snarled, "We'll see who learns a lesson, Wells!" Looking at the marshal, he said, "How about taking the cuffs off us, Claxton? The girl's daddy wants to fight me. You ought to let him!"

"I'd love it!" exclaimed Wells.

Parris was hoping his plan would work. All he needed was to get the handcuffs off. Being a resourceful man, he would find a way to get his hands on a gun.

Larry Mangrum stomped toward the bounty hunter, blind with fury. Before anyone could stop him, he moved up to Parris and delivered a savage blow to the bounty hunter's jaw. Parris went down, rolling in the dirt. Rising to his knees and shaking his head, he swore vehemently at Larry and said, "You stay out of this!"

Larry stepped up close and growled through his teeth,

"You touch Miss Molly again and I'll beat you to a pulp, Parris!"

"You got no say in what I do!" retorted the bounty hunter as he stood.

"Well, *I* do!" rasped Pete Wells, moving toward Parris again.

The marshal lunged for Wells, catching him by the shirt collar and halting him in his tracks. "That's enough of this!" bellowed Claxton. "No more fighting, do you hear? Nobody's cuffs are coming off!"

While Claxton was speaking, Larry's attention was drawn to him, and Parris took advantage of the moment by backing up a step and kicking the cowboy violently in the groin. Larry doubled over, groaning. Claxton swore at Parris, who was now preparing to kick Larry in the face. Ross Blake had seen enough. He dashed in and swung a rock-hard fist, connecting solidly with the bounty hunter's jaw. Parris went down hard and stayed there. He was out cold.

Turning to the others, Blake said, "We need to get going. Every minute we stay here, we make ourselves more vulnerable to the Sioux." To Claxton he said, "This bounty hunter is more trouble than he's worth. Take the cuffs off him, Marshal. He's staying here."

Looking a bit amazed, Hal Stacy said, "Ross . . . you mean you're just going to leave him out here alone?"

"The man's a menace, Hal," said Blake defensively. "I have these other passengers to think of. Their safety is uppermost in my mind. We've got enough problems with the Sioux, especially if we are now contending with Two Thumbs. Parris is an added hazard. He stays."

Smiling broadly, John Claxton said, "That suits me fine, Blake! I'll take the cuffs off him while the rest of you get back on the stage."

Larry Mangrum walked a little gingerly as he headed for the coach. Molly thanked him for being protective of her, as did Betty and Pete.

They were just about ready to go when Jack Parris came to and discovered his wrists were free. Rolling to a sitting position, he shook his head and blinked his eyes. At that moment Ross Blake snapped the reins, moving the stage away from the spot, and suddenly Parris realized what was happening. Laboring to stand up, he hollered, "Hey! Hey, Blake! Wait a minute! You can't be leaving me here!"

"Just watch me!" Blake called over his shoulder, making the horses pick up speed.

The bounty hunter struggled to his feet and began running after the stage. He was still dizzy, and after a few steps, he fell. As he rose again and began staggering after the stage, he shouted, "Blake! Please! Don't leave me here! The Sioux will find me! They'll kill me!"

"That would be a pity!" Blake said loudly.

Parris fell again, and tears began to spill from his eyes. Calling after the rolling stage, he bawled, "Blake, please! Those outlaws from the Hole may be coming after me! They'll kill me! If you leave me here, it's the same as murder! That makes you a murderer!"

Ross Blake had not intended to leave the man to die. He had wanted simply to scare some sense into him. He drew rein now, and as the coach came to a halt, he whipped around on the seat and looked at Parris, who was now stumbling toward him.

"Please, Blake!" wept Parris. "I'm sorry for the trouble I've made. I won't be any more of a problem. I promise!"

John Claxton came out of the coach. Looking up at Blake, he said with sand in his voice, "If he comes on this stage, it's cuffed exactly as he was!"

Drawing near, Parris choked out, "That's fine, Marshal! I won't be any more trouble. I promise!"

Jack Parris realized his chances at the five thousand dollars were almost nil. But he at least wanted to get out of this situation alive. He told himself, however, that if the opportunity presented itself before they met up with the cavalry, he would still try to kill the whole bunch and collect the reward money.

Parris was cuffed again and shoved into the coach by the marshal. As Claxton climbed in and shut the door, he looked sternly at the bounty hunter and grunted, "You stay away from the girl, you hear me?"

Parris nodded, lips pulled tight.

"You touch her again," warned Larry Mangrum, "and I'll cave in your mangy skull."

"You won't have to, Larry," put in Wells, burning Parris with hot eyes. "I'll kill him before you can get near him."

As the stage moved on over the uneven land, the sun made its arc across the sky. Canteens were passed among the passengers several times as the hot day wore on. With those next to the windows keeping sharp eyes on the surrounding terrain, the passengers turned their conversation to the optimistic note that by morning they would be at Deadman Butte under the protection of the cavalry. Betty Wells added that it was still possible the army would come looking for them. If so, their edge of safety would come even sooner.

When the sun had disappeared behind the western horizon, Ross Blake pulled the coach under a stand of cottonwood trees where a small brook babbled with cool, clear water. He and the shotgunner slid down from the box as the passengers began to file out.

"We'll spend the night here," said Blake. "You ladies can sleep inside the coach. Sorry I can't offer you a good hot meal. I have some beef jerky aboard, but for anything other than that, you'll have to wait until we reach the relay station at Deadman Butte. And I guarantee you that Mrs. Boatman will fix you a breakfast you'll never forget!"

"I'm just relieved we've made it this far without any more Indian trouble," said Betty. "How long will it take us to reach the Butte in the morning, Mr. Blake?"

"We're about two hours away," Blake replied. "I thought about pushing on this evening, but the horses are pretty tired."

Marshal John Claxton had just released Pete Wells from the doorpost. Speaking to Blake, he said, "Shouldn't the cavalry have met us by now? Certainly they should have figured something was wrong hours ago."

"I would think so," agreed Blake. Though he was a bit worried, he covered it by chuckling. "You never know about the army, though. They might just be sitting there waiting for us to show up. They are known for doing some pretty dumb things!"

"Yeah," laughed Claxton, making a stab at humor. "They made you a captain!"

Blake joined in the laughter. "You're right, there, Marshal. Like I said, they are known for doing some pretty dumb things!"

The rest of the group enjoyed the laugh with the two men. All, that is, except for Jack Parris.

Dawn came with the Wyoming sky crystal clear. The stagecoach was rolling southward when the sun sent its first yellow rays streaming across the land. There was concern among passengers and crew that no sign of the cavalry platoon had been seen.

After nearly two hours of traveling, Deadman Butte came into view, suddenly lifting its proud, rugged head some three thousand feet above the level of the grassy plain. Only minutes after Blake and Stacy first saw the Butte, Blake drew a quick breath and pulled back on the reins. When the vehicle came to a halt, Hal Stacy also saw the column of black smoke near the base of the Butte.

John Claxton stuck his head out the window and asked, "What's wrong, Blake? Why are we stopped?"

In a dead tone Blake replied, "The relay station is on fire."

Chapter Eight

Bent over in the saddle and grimacing with pain, outlaw Clyde Zimmerman guided his horse into the shallow valley that led into the hideout known as the Hole-in-the-Wall at the same time Ross Blake and the occupants of the stagecoach were studying the column of smoke many miles to the south.

Surrounded on all four sides by great soaring walls of red granite, the Hole was a virtual fortress. As soon as Zimmerman was in the shadows of the towering monoliths at the Hole's entrance, four riders came out of a rock enclosure and surrounded him. When they recognized the bent-over figure, they holstered their guns and signaled to other men hidden in the high rocks that all was okay.

As the riders pulled up, Zimmerman raised his head and said, "Smith and Mudd are dead."

"What happened?" asked one of the riders.

"I'll explain it later," Zimmerman answered, clutching his wounded shoulder. "I'd have been in before this, but I kept passin' out and fallin' from the saddle. Got a slug in my shoulder."

"We'll get you to old Abe Yonkers, Clyde," said another. "He's patched up a lot of the boys carryin' bullets. He's in his shack right now."

Gritting his teeth, Zimmerman said, "I gotta see Max Lund first."

"What for?" came the question from one of the four.

"Just help me get to him," Zimmerman said, clipping his words. "You can listen in."

One of the four took the reins from Zimmerman's hands and led his horse deeper into the Hole. Five minutes later they pulled up in front of the shack where Max Lund was staying.

"Max! Hey, Max!" called one of them. "Clyde Zimmerman's out here. He wants to see you!"

The door came open and a husky blond-headed German appeared. He was shirtless from the waist up, exposing his long johns over a muscular upper body. Lund took one look at Zimmerman and rushed to him. "Clyde, what happened? Where's Giff and Earl?"

"They're dead," the wounded man said.

Reaching toward Zimmerman, Lund said, "Here, let me help you. We'll get you over to Abe's shack. He'll take care of you."

"In a minute," choked out Zimmerman as the big German lifted him from the saddle and eased him to the ground. "There's somethin' I gotta tell you."

By this time outlaws were emerging from their rickety shacks and from the rope corral where their horses were kept. Max Lund laid his friend flat on his back and then called for someone to bring Abe Yonkers.

Zimmerman felt a wave of dizziness wash over him. When it passed, he looked up at Lund, who was now kneeling over him, and said, "I . . . I think I'm gonna pass out. Gotta tell you . . . about Jack Parris."

"Jack Parris!" exclaimed Lund. "You saw Jack Parris?"

"Yeah. Tried to bring him to you, but . . . but I got shot and . . . and Giff and Earl were killed."

Abe Yonkers, an aged, silver-haired outlaw, came and knelt beside Clyde Zimmerman as the wounded man slowly told the story of how he and his two friends had stumbled onto Jack Parris at Mayoworth and how they had tried to take him from the Rawlins-bound stagecoach. When Zimmerman had finished the story, he passed out.

Standing up, Lund said, "Couple of you boys carry Clyde over to Abe's shack so he can patch him up." As it was being done, the German ran his icy blue eyes over the crowd and barked, "All you boys hate bounty hunters, right?"

There was instant agreement.

With hatred showing on his round face, Max Lund said, "You boys have heard me tell about Jack Parris, the bounty hunter who got the drop on me and put me behind bars."

The outlaws nodded and spoke words affirming that they remembered.

"Well, now's my chance to get Parris!" blustered Lund, doubling up his fists and shaking them. "I need a dozen men to ride with me and help me take that scaly snake off the stage." Lund had his dozen volunteers within seconds. "Okay, boys." The German grinned. "Get yourselves ready. We ride in half an hour!"

The six horses in the stagecoach team, exhausted from their long haul the day before, fought their bits and snorted in rebellion as Ross Blake forced them toward the grisly scene that lay before them at the base of Deadman Butte. The animals seemed to sense the violence and bloodshed that had taken place there.

A cold hand of fear gripped the occupants of the coach as they saw the scattered bodies of soldiers and horses. Blake drew up in front of what was left of the way station house. The roof had collapsed in the fire, leaving only portions of the blackened walls standing. The larger timbers were still burning. The charred remains of two bodies, most likely Walt and Florence Boatman, the stationmaster and his wife, lay near the smoldering doorjamb.

Hal Stacy made a gagging sound deep in his throat as he

scanned the horrid sight. As Blake climbed down from the box and the stage doors were coming open, he said, "Don't let the women come out here!"

Claxton released Pete Wells from the doorpost, quickly shackling his wrists together. Mother and daughter remained inside the coach as the men filed out. The faces of the two women were rigid as they clung to each other, purposely keeping their eyes away from the windows.

As the other men drew up beside him, Ross Blake stood immobile. His stomach wrenched and his shoulders drooped as he viewed the ghastly scene. Twenty-four mangled bodies, naked and bloody, lay in the blaring light of the sun. Their scalps had been taken, their bodies savagely mutilated.

Swallowing bile, Blake said, "Some of those men were butchered up before they died. You can tell by the amount of blood around their bodies. This looks like the work of Two Thumbs."

John Claxton ejected a profane oath. His face was pale and drawn, his brow beaded with icy sweat. "We'd better keep moving, Blake," he said, sleeving away the sweat.

"Yeah, Blake," said Jack Parris. "The best thing for us to do is climb back on that stage and put the horses in a dead run."

"If we did that we'd never make it the twelve miles to Arminto," Blake responded. "The horses need rest and water. Our best bet is to take care of them and then get to Arminto as fast as possible."

Blake continued to study the scene before him. Solemnly he said, "The Sioux must have caught the platoon by surprise. Probably came from around the Butte just as they were riding in. All of them are right out in the open." Pointing to the huge mass of jumbled rocks and boulders that lay at the southern base of Deadman Butte, he added, "If they'd had time to get in among those rocks, they could have held the Indians off for a long time."

"You're right," agreed Pete Wells. "But it appears the

Sioux took a pretty good licking before they killed all the soldiers. Look how many dead pintos there are among the army horses. And you can see a lot of bloody spots where bodies were picked up."

"They paid a pretty healthy price," nodded Blake. "But there's something odd here."

"What's that?" asked Larry Mangrum.

Holding his gaze on the awful spectacle of death, Blake replied, "This platoon was made up of two squads of a dozen men each. There would have been one officer to lead them, most likely a lieutenant. That would make twenty-five men. I only see twenty-four out there. One is missing."

"Maybe the Indians let one live and took him with them," suggested Pete Wells.

"Not likely," said Blake. "Let's look around those rocks at the base of the Butte."

"I'll climb up on one of the boulders and keep a lookout while you and the others look among the rocks, Ross," volunteered Hal Stacy.

"Good." Blake nodded. To the other men he said, "Come on, fellas. There has to be another man around here somewhere."

As Larry, Claxton, Wells, and Parris moved in among the rocks and boulders, Blake stepped to the coach. Looking through a window at mother and daughter, he said, "Ladies, there should be one more body out there. We're trying to find it. I—"

"Mr. Blake!" came Larry Mangrum's voice from somewhere in the jumble of massive rocks.

"Excuse me, ladies," said Blake. Turning toward the rocks, he called, "Yeah?"

At that moment Larry Mangrum appeared at the edge of the rocks. "There's a man back here! He's still alive!"

Within seconds every man except Hal Stacy had gathered at a shaded spot among the boulders where a young corporal lay dying. He was still clothed. Blake, kneeling down beside him, laid a hand on his shoulder. The corporal's eyes were closed, but there was a slight rise and fall of his chest. Blood bubbled from around an arrow that was imbedded deep in his abdomen. The shaft had been broken off, leaving it protruding some three or four inches from his body. He had a bullet hole in his left shoulder, and one in his right thigh. It was evident he was bleeding to death.

"I'll get him some water," said Larry Mangrum, and he disappeared.

Squeezing the dying man's shoulder, Blake said, "Corporal, can you hear me?"

The bleeding soldier stirred slightly.

"Corporal, we're your friends. Can you hear me?"

Glassy eyes appeared under fluttering lids. The corporal worked his jaw, then ran a dry tongue over equally dry lips. He swallowed hard, trying to focus on Blake's face. Faintly he uttered, "I . . . I hear you. Who are you?"

"My name's Blake. I'm driving the stagecoach your detachment was to escort to Rawlins."

Gritting his teeth in pain, then relaxing somewhat, the bleeding man said, "I'm . . . Jeff Morrison. They . . . they ambushed us. We didn't have . . . a chance. I . . . I crawled in here during the battle. Are any of the men . . . are they—?"

"They're all dead, Morrison," Blake said evenly.

John Claxton bent low and said, "Corporal, can you tell us if Two Thumbs was leading them?"

Morrison closed his eyes and then opened them again. "Yes. It was Two Thumbs."

Claxton's features became grim, and his cheeks went white.

"I thought so," Ross Blake said through tight lips.

At that instant Larry Mangrum appeared, bearing a canteen. On his heels were Betty and Molly Wells. Larry caught the look of horror on the faces of the four men. "What's the matter?" he queried.

Blake answered, "The corporal says the attack was led by Two Thumbs."

The news washed over the cowboy like cold water.

"Marshal Claxton," Betty said to the lawman, "if we have to battle Two Thumbs, it seems to me you'd be smart to give us all guns."

Claxton did not comment.

Wells said, "Betty, you two shouldn't have left the coach."

"I thought maybe we could help," she countered. "I didn't want to leave Molly in the coach alone."

Molly took the canteen from Larry's hand and knelt down beside Ross Blake. Removing the cap, she put the canteen to the dying soldier's lips and said, "Here, Corporal. Let's get some water into you."

Morrison lined his sight on her lovely face and tried to smile. "Thank you, ma'am," he breathed.

Blake stood up and said to the men, "Let's let the women look after him for a while."

Jack Parris showed a pallor beneath the tan of his craggy face. Deep in his eyes lay the shadow of a strong fear, which was evident as he said shakily, "Blake, we gotta get to Arminto. Two Thumbs might come back, and then where would we be?"

Eyes glum, Blake pointed with his head for the men to follow him. They weaved their way out into the open, and then Blake said to Parris, "I thought I made myself clear. We aren't going anywhere until those horses are rested. To do otherwise would be suicide."

Parris stood breathing hard, but no answer came from his wire-thin lips.

Blake looked up at Hal Stacy, who was still positioned on top of one of the tall boulders. "See anything, Hal?"

"Nothing moving but a few antelope to the east," came Stacy's reply. "What's the story? Larry said the trooper's shot up pretty bad."

"He's about done for," responded Blake. "The women

are with him." Turning to the others, he said, "Since we're going to be here awhile, I think we ought to do something about all those bodies."

"You mean bury them?" asked Parris.

"We won't have time to do that," said Blake. "But at least we could drag them off the field and pile them over on the other side of the boulders. Maybe cover them with rocks. Give them some kind of burial, at least."

"Seems like the decent thing to do," said Claxton.

The thought of handling the bloody, mutilated bodies was not a pleasant thing to any of them, but it was agreed that it should be done. Jack Parris was about to protest when Pete Wells asked the marshal if his cuffs could be removed so he could be unencumbered while doing his part.

Claxton ran his gaze over the field of naked, crumpled corpses. There were no rifles anywhere in sight. "It looks like the Sioux took all of the guns, Wells, so I guess it would be all right." Reaching for the key in his pocket, he added, "The cuffs go back on as soon as we're done. Understand?"

Pete Wells nodded. Instantly, Jack Parris realized this could be his opportunity. Turning to Claxton he said, "How about me, Marshal? Can I have my cuffs off also?"

"Yep." Claxton nodded. "Same goes for you, too, though as soon as we're finished, the cuffs go back on."

"Whatever you say," Parris said, bobbing his head.

"All right, let's get to it," Blake said, lifting his hat and palming sweat from his brow. To his shotgunner on top of the boulder, he called, "Hal, keep your eyes peeled. I'm going to pull the stage into that big gap over there between those two boulders. If the Sioux should show up, it'll be protected. And we'll have a better chance than the troopers did. We can get into the rocks for protection."

Pete Wells and Jack Parris rubbed their wrists as the handcuffs came off, and the five men began the gruesome task of removing the bodies from the open field to the west side of the jumbled rock pile. Each man picked out a corpse, took hold of the ankles, and began dragging it around the edge of the rock pile. The limp bodies made smooth grooves in the soft earth. Blake commented that they had probably been attacked the previous afternoon, judging from the condition of the corpses. The Indians must have picked up their dead and stayed at the spot all night, then set fire to the station before they pulled out this morning.

While doing his portion of the work, Jack Parris concentrated on one thing. Now that his wrists were free, he had to find a way to get his hands on a gun. He returned from the rocks to lay hold of his fourth corpse, and as he bent over to get a grip on the ankles, something black and shiny caught his eye. It was protruding from the left side of the body, which was lying facedown. Suddenly he realized what the dark object was. This must have been the officer in charge of the platoon. Tattered ribbons of blue uniform lay nearby. Somehow the officer had fallen on top of his holster.

Parris shot a glance toward the other men, each busy with his own hideous task. No one was looking in the bounty hunter's direction. Parris quickly knelt down and slipped the holster from under the body. Green-bodied flies were massed around the wounds, especially where the scalp had been lifted. The revolver was still in its blood-covered holster. As if to use the blistering heat for an excuse, Parris pulled out his shirttail, letting it dangle over the belt line of his trousers.

Making sure once more that no one was looking his way, the bounty hunter removed the gun from the holster and jammed it under his belt. He tossed the holster on the heap of blue rags and then stood up and began dragging the body toward the boulders, satisfied that his loose shirt properly covered the handle of the gun. All he had to do now was choose his time. If he killed the five men first, he could use one of their guns to help finish off the women.

His whole frame tingled with excitement. It was as though the gods had predestined him to find the body of the officer. The five thousand dollars would be his after all!

As the sun lifted higher in the sky, the shade grew thinner amid the boulders where the two women attended to Corporal Jeff Morrison. The dying man roused to consciousness periodically, only to pass out once again. While Betty gave him sips of water, Molly bathed his brow with a wet handkerchief.

The young blond woman said, "Mother, will . . . the men kill you and me if they see Two Thumbs is going to get us?"

"Let's not think about that right now, honey," said Betty. "We must keep our minds on surviving."

"But I've heard what Two Thumbs does to white women, Mother. I'd rather die than—"

"Molly, that's enough of that kind of talk. Now let's concentrate on making this young man as comfortable as possible."

Morrison opened his eyes and coughed. His body shook for a moment and then relaxed.

Molly cradled the young man's head in her hands and said softly, "Corporal, is there anything I can do for you?"

Morrison's eyelids fluttered open as he said, "My wife . . . Tell her I . . . I love her. She lives in Casper."

With tears in her eyes, Molly looked gently down at the young corporal and whispered, "I'll tell her. I promise."

With that, he lapsed back into unconsciousness.

Molly took a wet handkerchief from her mother and placed it on Morrison's fevered brow. After several minutes of silence, Molly said, "Mother, would God hold it against Larry for having been a gunfighter, since he's changed and has been trying to make something productive of his life?"

Betty looked at her daughter blankly. "I don't know if I understand what you're getting at."

Molly's pretty face pinched. "Well, what I mean is, there just doesn't seem to be any way for Larry to evade his showdown with Vic Spain. Not long ago, Pastor Perkins said that man's extremities are God's possibilities."

"Yes, he did," Betty replied softly.

"Then would I be out of line to pray for a way for Larry to get out of his showdown with Spain? I mean, especially since Larry has changed the direction of his life?"

Betty smiled at her daughter. "You are quite fond of Larry, aren't you, honey?"

"It's more than fondness, Mother," said Molly. "I've fallen in love with him."

The mother raised her eyebrows. "A bit sudden, isn't it?"

"Maybe a little bit, but nonetheless real."

"Do you think he feels the same way about you?"

"Yes."

"Has he told you so?"

"Not in so many words, but I can read it in his eyes."

Betty looked back at Morrison, who was stirring again.

"You didn't answer my question, Mother," said Molly. "In Larry's case, man's extremities seem to have run out."

Patting her daughter's arm, the mother said, "You wouldn't be out of line at all, honey. You go ahead and pray for that. I'll help you. And while we're at it, we'd better ask God to get us out of here before we meet up with Two Thumbs. Or the other won't matter."

By early afternoon the unpleasant job of giving the bodies a rock burial was finished. Hunger was beginning to take its toll on the group, but they now knew they would not see a meal until they got to Arminto. There was plenty of water, so they filled their stomachs with it.

Jack Parris knew he would have to make his move

quickly. At the moment Marshal Claxton was taking his fill of water, but when he finished, the handcuffs would go back on. Parris would have to act when all five men were in one spot. Hal Stacy had come down off the boulder to take a drink, but Ross Blake had gone in the rocks to see about the corporal.

Stacy was still taking water from a canteen when Claxton set his down and said, "Okay, Pete, you first. On with the cuffs."

Parris's heart began to throb. He did not dare pull his gun and start shooting until he had all five men together. The women would not matter, because they were not armed. But he had to have Blake out from those rocks!

The ratchets made their clicking sound as the handcuffs closed on the wrists of Pete Wells. Pulling the second pair from his hip pocket, Claxton turned toward Parris. Suddenly Ross Blake emerged from the rocks saying, "Morrison's about gone, fellas. He's—"

Jack Parris made his move. Whipping out the revolver from under his shirt, he yelled, "Everybody get your hands up!"

John Claxton halted in his tracks, shock framing his face.

Parris, standing twenty feet from the group, suddenly decided it would be best to have guns in both hands before he started shooting. While each man stood with his hands elevated, the bounty hunter snapped, "Claxton! Reach down real slow and take your gun from the holster with the tips of your fingers. Toss it to me. Move too quick and you're a dead man!"

"Where did you get that gun?" demanded Claxton.

"Did you hear me?" hissed Parris. "Give me your revolver, or I'll shoot you down like a cur dog!"

From their place among the rocks, Betty and Molly heard what was being said by Parris and Claxton. Both stood up beside the dying corporal. "That bounty hunter has gotten hold of a gun!" whispered Betty. "He'll take your father with him—maybe kill him!"

"What can we do?" whispered Molly in return.

Betty pressed her fingertips to her temples. "I don't know, honey. We've got to think of something!"

At the tense scene beside the rocks, Ross Blake, his years in the military having honed his mental perception to a sharp point, had guessed immediately what Jack Parris was planning to do. He was going to take Pete Wells in for the bounty on his head. In order to do it, he would have to kill everyone here, and Pete Wells, too.

Just then Blake noticed that John Claxton was slowly lowering his hand toward the butt of his revolver. Just as the marshal's fingertips touched the butt of his revolver, Blake said, "Marshal, can't you see what he's doing?"

"Shut up!" Parris snarled, staring hard at Blake. The bounty hunter would have shot Blake down, but Claxton, Larry, and Stacy still had their sidearms in their holsters, making it too dangerous. He had to disarm them first.

Larry Mangrum, his hands held up at head level, saw what was happening and knew they would all be dead men once Parris got a second gun. He wondered if he could drop his right hand, draw, and shoot Parris before the man could cut him down. He realized there was no choice; he had to try.

He looked at Jack Parris, whose face was a mask of fury. The greedy bounty hunter glared hotly at Blake and snapped, "So you think you're smart, don't you, Blake? Got it all figured out, huh?"

"Yeah," clipped Blake. "Kill all of us and carry Pete's body to the authorities at Rawlins, telling them some tall tale about what happened to us."

The bounty hunter's features became stony. Through colorless lips he growled, "That reward money is gonna be mine! Nothing and nobody is gonna stop me! I was planning on killing lover-boy Mangrum first, Blake, but now it's gonna be you!"

"You'll never get all of us, Parris," rasped Blake. "Some of us will draw on you before you can get us."

"Well, you're going first, Blake," Parris said jaggedly, "so you'll never know how it turns out, will you?" Flicking his hot eyes to the marshal, he blared, "Toss your gun to me, Claxton, or you'll die ahead of Blake!"

Larry Mangrum knew he could wait no longer. His right hand darted downward. At the same instant, he glimpsed the two women from the corner of his eye, creeping around the corner of a boulder. Suddenly they were throwing fist-sized rocks at Parris, and he started to turn his gun toward them—but he was too late. Larry's gun roared, the slug catching the bounty hunter in the shoulder, spinning him around and dropping him. The rocks sailed past him.

Like a hungry cat leaping on a mouse, Ross Blake pounced on Parris, wrenching the gun from his hand. Though Parris was wounded, he fought back. In the heat of the moment, Blake swung the butt of the revolver at the bounty hunter's mouth; his lips split, and several shattered teeth flew out. The bounty hunter growled furiously, almost like an animal, and Blake came down violently with the gun butt again. Parris went limp. He was out cold.

The marshal quickly handcuffed the unconscious man and examined the shoulder wound. The bullet had passed through the meaty part of the arm where it joins the shoulder, so no bone was touched. Claxton asked Betty Wells if she would bandage him up. Reluctantly, she began doing so, ripping off the opposite sleeve to use as a bandage. Pete Wells knelt down beside her.

Ross Blake stuck the service revolver under his belt and turned to Molly. "How's the corporal doing?" he asked.

"Not good," she answered, glancing at Larry Mangrum, who gave her a smile. "His periods of consciousness are getting farther apart."

Molly headed back into the rocks, followed by Blake

and Larry, while Hal Stacy made his way toward the
tallest boulder and scurried to its top, scouring the hori
zon for any movement.

After Jack Parris was bandaged up, the marshal carried
him to the stagecoach and laid him inside. The wounded
bounty hunter's hands were again cuffed behind his back
and Claxton used a length of rope to bind his ankles
together.

While Hal Stacy stayed in his lookout position, the
others attended to Corporal Jeff Morrison as the afternoon
sun ran its course down the western sky. Just before
sunset, the wounded soldier died. Blake, Larry, Claxton
and Wells gave him a rock burial near the other cavalry
men. As soon as they finished, they rounded the rock pile
and Blake said to the group, "Let's get on the stage and
head for Arminto. It'll be dark soon, but we can be there
in less than two hours."

From his place atop the boulder, Hal Stacy said loudly
"I don't think we're going anywhere, Ross."

Blake swung his gaze to the shotgunner and saw him
pointing southward. The others followed Stacy's finger. At
the crest of a gentle rise a half-mile south, a string of
mounted warriors was visible in the dim light of the dying
day.

Molly gasped, putting her hand to her mouth. Larry
Mangrum moved close to her as Wells laid his shackled
hands on Betty's shoulders. Every eye in the group was
riveted on the redskinned horsemen who sat erect on the
backs of their mounts, silhouetted against the darkening
sky.

Ross Blake adjusted the hat on his head and said in a
dismal tone, "Looks like we'll have to make our stand
right here, come sunup."

Chapter Nine

Deadman Butte thrust its rugged head into the darkening sky as the shadows of night moved across the land. The passengers and crew of the Rawlins-bound stagecoach stood together, watching the line of Sioux warriors until their forms were obscured by darkness. Ross Blake's voice broke the silence. "I counted twenty of them."

"Me, too," said Pete Wells.

"Do you really think they will wait till morning to attack us, Mr. Blake?" asked Betty.

"Yes," came Blake's reply. "They would be foolish to come at us at night. We can fight them from the rocks, and they know we'll be hard to hit. The moon will be out soon. We would be able to see them, but they would have a hard time seeing us. They won't come until morning."

"Do you think Two Thumbs is in that bunch?" asked Claxton.

"Since he was here for yesterday's massacre, I would say he is leading them," responded Blake. "He may not be showing us all his troops, but if he *is* down to twenty warriors, the platoon whittled down his followers pretty well before they died."

"Why did they let us see them?" asked Molly. "Why didn't they just wait and hit us with a surprise attack in

the morning? Wouldn't we be much more vulnerable while
traveling out in the open?"

Blake looked toward Molly's dark figure. "Yes, we would.
But you have to understand that Two Thumbs and his
warriors enjoy using scare tactics. They want us to lie
awake all night, dreading the attack that is coming in the
morning."

"They know they have us well outnumbered," put in
Larry Mangrum. "So they're not afraid to risk fighting us
while we take cover in the rocks."

"Right," agreed Blake. "But we're going to cut down
those odds a little bit. In the morning we're giving Betty
and Molly rifles."

"Now wait a minute!" blustered Claxton. "You can't—"

"I'm not going to argue, Marshal!" cut in Blake. "These
two women are not going to aim their guns at you. They
have a right to defend themselves against the Sioux, and
I'm giving them rifles."

"Now look here!" boomed the lawman.

"No, you look here," Blake ordered. "These passengers
are my responsibility, and I'm seeing to it they have all
the protection possible. Betty and Molly are not your
prisoners. They're getting guns in the morning."

Turning to the shadowed forms of the two women,
Blake said, "Ladies, I want you to wear men's hats and fire
from the rocks, staying very low. If the Indians recognize
you as females, they'll double their efforts to move in."

"Whatever you say," replied Betty, gloating inside that
the big lawman had been put in his place.

Pete Wells said to Claxton, "Marshal, I'm asking you
again. Please take my cuffs off when the Indians come in
the morning, and let me have a rifle."

Claxton was already angered by Ross Blake's stubborn-
ness, but Pete's insistence on getting his hands on a gun
caused the marshal's temper to soar. "No outlaw I've
arrested is going to be given a gun!" he barked.

Ross Blake felt his own temper flare. Speaking sharply,

he said, "Claxton, we've got Two Thumbs out there planning to come at us in the morning! *Two Thumbs!* His
warriors are twice as deadly as any other Sioux warriors,
and if they can take any of us alive, we'll wish we'd
committed suicide!"

Claxton moved close to Blake. With hot breath, he said,
"If you had ever worn a badge, you'd know better than to
ever put a gun in the hands of a killer."

Wells said, "I told you before, Marshal. I am not a
killer. I robbed people, yes, and I am very sorry about it.
But I never killed anyone, and I am not going to shoot you
in the back."

"You're right about that!" said Claxton. "Because you're
not getting a gun!"

Betty Wells was already nervous and edgy, but Claxton's
attitude toward her husband raked her temper raw. Fire
seemed to ignite within her breast as she turned toward
his bulky form in the dark. "Claxton!" she spat. "Pete
would have to be a fool to gun you down in front of these
other men!"

"What's to keep him from shooting me during the battle
with the Indians?" the marshal snapped back. "Who would
even see it? He'd just let the rest of you think the Indians
got me!"

Betty's anger drove her over to where the lawman stood.
Catching Claxton off guard, she pounded on his chest,
screaming, "You're stubborn and bullheaded! That tin star
has muddled your brain!"

"Betty!" Pete shouted, moving in. "Stop it! This isn't
going to help!"

At the same instant, Claxton seized the angry woman's
wrists. She pulled against his hands, but his strength was
too great. Then Pete Wells stepped in, separating the
marshal from Betty. Taking hold of his wife by the arm
and pulling her back, he said in a level tone, "Honey, get
hold of yourself."

Betty, not resisting her husband, stood there breathing

hard and glaring at the marshal, who was somewhat dazed from the woman's attack. Claxton had turned away and was mumbling when Ross Blake stepped close and said, "Marshal, Betty's right. Even if Pete were a killer, he'd have a pretty hard time taking Hal, Larry, and myself out without getting shot himself. Besides, do you really think he would commit murder with his wife and daughter present?"

No comment came from Claxton.

"Think of it this way, Marshal," Wells spoke up. "With all these savage Indians around, wouldn't I be mighty stupid to kill you and these other men? The only hope any of us have of getting out of this mess alive is to stick together. What kind of chance would my family and I have trying to get out of here alone?"

The moon was putting in an appearance on the eastern horizon.

"He's right, Marshal," Blake continued. "We need Pete with a gun in his hands. If I were in your boots, I'd rather take a chance on Pete than on having those Indians kill me."

Before Claxton could react, Larry Mangrum said, "I know you look at me as just a green kid, Marshal Claxton, but I have to agree with Mr. Blake. I say give Mr. Wells a gun."

"We're going to need all the firepower we can muster," Hal Stacy added.

As the moon rose, its yellow light casting shadows on the ground, Marshal Claxton took a deep breath, pursed his lips, and let it out slowly. Shaking his head, he said, "Okay. This goes against every fiber of my being, but I'm giving in to the majority. If the cuffs are coming off, they might as well come off right now." Pulling the key from his pocket, Claxton stepped up to Wells and began unlocking the handcuffs, mumbling, "Folks in this crowd should have been Philadelphia lawyers."

Betty touched Claxton's arm. "Thank you, Marshal,"

she said softly. "I'm sorry I lost my temper. Forgive me, please."

The marshal chuckled as he squeezed the handcuffs closed and dropped them into his hip pocket. "Ma'am, I hope you'll show those Indians some of that temper tomorrow!" he declared.

The marshal went to the stagecoach to check on Jack Parris, who was awake and in a sour mood. His bleeding had stopped, but the pain in his shoulder was severe. Claxton gave him water and then left him to sulk in the coach.

When he returned to the group, they were discussing their hunger. "Blake," Claxton said, "you don't suppose the meat on those dead horses out there would still be good?"

"I doubt it," replied Blake. "It was plenty hot today, and those animals have probably been dead for at least twenty-six hours."

"Being hungry isn't as bad as being sick with food poisoning," put in Molly Wells.

"Can't disagree with that," Claxton replied.

"So we keep drinking water," said Ross Blake. "Now, let's talk about how we're going to handle the attack tomorrow. I want to get the stage and the team farther back in the rocks. I'm planning on us coming out of this thing alive, and we're going to need the stage and the horses to get us on to Arminto and Rawlins. We need to protect them as much as possible. Marshal, I suggest that you actually cuff Parris to the stage. That will save us any worries about him."

"I couldn't agree more," said Claxton.

Running his gaze between the two younger men, Blake said, "Hal, you and Larry move the stage deeper into the rocks, then take the rifles and ammunition down from the rack. Break out the rifles and let the ladies get the feel of them. The rest of us can use them, too. We'll plan each person's fighting position and equip it with plenty of ammunition. I want Betty and Molly well fortified and in spots where they can stay comfortably low for shooting. We dare not let Two Thumbs know we have women here."

"I think your idea to have them wear our hats is good, Ross," Pete Wells put in. "As long as the Indians don't get right in here with us, they'll never suspect the truth. Betty can have my hat. If one of you gentlemen would let Molly—"

"She can wear mine," spoke up Larry Mangrum.

Molly turned and smiled at him, causing Larry's heart to skip a beat.

A note of optimism in his voice, Ross Blake said, "I'm hoping that the nineteen men we saw with Two Thumbs is all he has. If so, we've got a decent chance of getting through this alive. With some good shooting, maybe we can whittle them down and send them running."

"We're going to do it, Ross," piped up Hal Stacy. "I just know it."

"That's the spirit." Blake smiled. "Let's all of us keep a positive attitude about it."

"I'm not throwing cold water," said Claxton, "but maybe we'd best decide on what to do if the savages are able to overpower us and come into the rocks. I'm talking about Betty and Molly. You . . . you know what I mean. I'm saying if . . . well, if—"

"What you're wondering, Marshal," Molly said, "is whether one of the surviving men should do a mercy killing on Mother and me if it comes down to it."

"Yeah," nodded the bulky lawman. "That's what I was trying to say."

Molly looked at her mother and then said, "This is a difficult thing to consider, but I believe we would both rather die at one of your hands than go through what the Sioux would do to us before they killed us anyway."

"That's right," said Betty, running her gaze over the faces of the men. "If it should come to that, please don't let Molly and me be taken by the Sioux." Her eyes came to rest on the face of her husband. "Pete, please don't let them take us."

Pete Wells swallowed hard, closing his eyes. Opening them, he looked her straight in the eye and said with difficulty, "I won't."

Betty looked solemnly at the other men. "It is agreed, then, gentlemen? You won't allow the Indians to capture my daughter and me?"

Each of the four men nodded silently.

Under Ross Blake's directions, the group made preparations for the impending attack. Each person was assigned his or her battle position. Pete Wells and Larry Mangrum would be closest to the women, flanking them on each side. The rifles were handed out, along with ammunition, and Blake gave pointers on Indian fighting, schooling his passengers and shotgunner as best he could.

With everything settled and in place, the group milled around in the moonlight, attempting to keep their thoughts off their empty stomachs. Betty and Pete Wells sat together on a two-foot-high rock and talked quietly. The marshal, Ross Blake, and Hal Stacy sat on the ground and talked, while Larry helped Molly climb up on the tall boulder that Stacy had used for a lookout post. They sat down together and quietly took in the beauty of the land by moonlight.

The night breeze plucked at Molly's hair. Larry wanted to touch it but restrained himself. Molly sniffed the cool air and said, "It's so peaceful, Larry. Seems hard to believe that in a few hours this place will be filled with violence. I wish it could just stay like this."

"Me, too, Miss Molly," agreed the cowboy. "I'd be satisfied to sit right here with you forever."

Mangrum's words sent a warm tingle through Molly's heart. Looking at him, she said, "Do you really mean that?"

"I sure do, Miss Molly," he said softly.

A tender smile played on her full red lips. "You can call me Molly. The 'miss' sounds so formal."

"All right, Molly," he said, returning the smile. He wanted so desperately to take her into his arms and tell her that he had fallen in love with her, but he told himself it would be pointless. She liked him a lot, he could tell, but falling in love with him would probably take more time—and time was something they did not have. Even if they did make it through the tight spot they were in right now, he would die the day they arrived in Rawlins. *Why should I complicate Molly's life by giving her the knowledge that a man who will die shortly is in love with her?* he reasoned.

Molly lifted her gaze skyward, where the big silver moon was sailing higher through the black sea of night, fading the stars that closely surrounded its aura of light. The breeze continued to toy with her long blond hair.

"Gorgeous sight, isn't it?" Larry half whispered.

"There are really no words to describe it," she answered. Then she pulled her gaze from the sky to look at his face with a grave expression.

Larry studied the worry on her features. "You're frightened about tomorrow, aren't you?"

"In one way I am."

"What do you mean—in one way?"

He saw tears fill her deep-blue eyes. Impulsively, he reached out to touch her hand. She quickly laid her other hand on top of his and squeezed it, and then bent her head and used her upper hand to brush an unruly lock of hair from her forehead.

"Molly, what is it?" he asked tenderly. Then he felt the warm tears drop on his hand. "Molly . . . ?"

She lifted her head and looked at him through the watery film. "Larry, tomorrow may be our last day on earth. I . . . I want to ask you something."

Larry felt his throat go tight. "Yes?"

"Yesterday when those outlaws wanted to take Mother

and me with them, and you risked your life and killed that one to stop them, do you remember what happened?"

"You mean when you laid your hand on my arm and told me it meant a lot that I cared what happened to you?"

"I mean what happened after that."

"When we looked into each other's eyes?"

"Yes."

For Larry Mangrum there was a feeling like a wild wind rushing through him. That had been the moment he knew he had fallen in love with her. Was she about to say that the same thing had happened in her own heart? He paused a moment before answering. Should he tell her the truth? Maybe it would be better not to, yet they both could die tomorrow. Suddenly he knew it was right to tell her. "Molly, are you asking me if something special happened to me at that moment?"

"Yes, Larry. Did it?"

"It did," he answered with conviction. "I wasn't going to tell you because of what is going to happen when we get to Rawlins, but now I want you to know. I knew I was in love with you at that moment, Molly."

"Oh, Larry," she breathed, raising her free hand to stroke his face. "That's when I fell in love with you!"

The stars seemed to desert the sky and nestle in Molly's eyes. There was a magnetism between them, and both knew it would be useless to resist. Larry flicked a glance at the group below; no one was watching Molly and him. Reaching toward her face, he cupped it in his hands, smoothing away the tears with his thumbs. She closed her eyes and gave him her lips. The kiss was tender, silky, and sweet.

When their lips parted, they looked longingly into each other's eyes and then kissed again. Larry folded her into his arms and held her tight for a long moment. When he released her, she looked at him misty eyed and said, "Oh, Larry, we must have our life together! We can't fall in love like this and let it end tomorrow, or in a few days."

Larry wanted to tell Molly everything was going to be all right—that they *would* have their life together—but it would have been a lie. Even if they survived the Indian attack tomorrow, Vic Spain was waiting.

"Larry," she said, gripping his hands, "If somehow we do live through this ordeal tomorrow, you must promise me that you won't go to Rawlins to face Vic Spain. I love you, and if you love me as you say you do, you'll want to live so we can have a lifetime together."

Larry Mangrum agonized over his dilemma. He was in love with Molly Wells; indeed, he would have liked nothing better than to marry her and spend his life as her husband. But he knew he would have to look in the mirror every morning for the rest of his life, and he could not stand looking at a man who had been responsible for pain and injury to others. He could not stand looking at a coward.

Speaking softly, he explained his feelings to Molly.

Reacting from the heart of a woman in love, Molly said, "Larry, I can't speak for your parents, but I think they would rather have you avoid facing Spain to stay alive than ending up in a cold grave. As for me, I have seen enough already to know that you are no coward. And I think if the law in Rawlins were to be alerted that Spain has threatened to hurt your parents or other people, they could warn Spain of the consequences if he did it."

Their hands were still locked together. With a shaky voice, Larry said, "Molly, you just don't understand men like Vic Spain. Nothing would stop him from carrying out his threat. He has no respect for the law. Molly, I want to marry you and spend my life with you more than I have ever wanted anything in the world. But I'm in a trap. There is no way out. I have to face Spain."

Molly let go of his hands and brushed at the locks of hair that the breeze had toppled over her eyes. "Then at least stay away from Rawlins until you have time to practice and get faster than Spain is."

Larry chuckled dryly. "It would take years for me to become faster than Vic Spain, Molly. The only way it could happen would be for him to get old and slow down. I could never match him while he's in his prime. A lot of men have tried it, and all of them are now six feet under."

The beautiful young woman bit down on her lower lip, then said, "I believe there's still a way to save your life."

He looked at her with mild speculation. "And that is?"

Lifting her eyes skyward, she said, "Do you really believe in the God your father serves?"

"Yes, of course I do."

"Well, I've already started praying to Him about this situation. He will work a way."

Larry's face twisted. "Molly, I . . . I haven't been too religious. I'm not sure that's going to work in my case."

"Oh, yes it is," she retorted. "God cares about you. I'm praying that something will happen to prevent you from facing Spain."

Glumly, Larry said, "Yeah, maybe I'll die tomorrow with a Sioux arrow in me." He shook his head and then, running his fingers through his black, curly hair, said quickly, "I'm sorry, Molly. I just—"

"I love you, Larry Mangrum," Molly said, setting her jaw.

"I love you, too, beautiful lady," he said, looking deeply into her eyes. "I admire your faith and appreciate your prayers." Pulling her to him, he kissed her again.

They slid off the boulder and returned to the others, who were preparing to bed down for the night. When everyone else was settled down, Ross Blake went to where Larry Mangrum was stretched out on the ground and whispered, "Hey, kid, can we talk?"

"Sure," Larry said, rising up on an elbow.

"Let's take a walk."

The two men made their way in the moonlight to a spot amid the rocks about fifty feet from where the group was bedded down. Looking straight at the younger man, Blake said, "This thing about you and Spain is eating at my insides, Larry. Why don't you let me precede you into town and see what I can do about getting him run off?"

"I appreciate your concern, Mr. Blake," Larry said, "but we've already been over that. It won't work."

"I've watched you and Molly together. You two are more than friends, aren't you?"

The handsome cowboy paused a moment and then nodded. "Yes, sir. We are. I tried to keep it from happening, but it just did."

"Are you really in love with her?"

"Totally."

Satisfied he had a good leverage with which to work, Blake said, "Then, kid, you've got everything to live for. Don't throw it away because of foolish pride."

Larry shook his head. "It's not pride," he argued. "It's the cold hard fact that I can't let innocent people be hurt by my inaction. Furthermore, I hate a coward, and I would hate cowardice in myself a thousand times more than in some other man. If I don't have the showdown with Spain, I'll have no respect for myself, and I certainly won't have the right to ask a wonderful woman like Molly to marry me."

Blake scrubbed a palm over his angular face. "You won't let me at least go ahead of you into town and try to get Spain run off?"

"Mr. Blake, I appreciate what you're trying to do, but Spain would only hurt somebody in retaliation. I can't take that chance."

Blake shrugged his wide shoulders. "Okay, kid. You'd better get some sleep. Big day tomorrow."

Larry bid Blake good night and returned to the spot where he had bedded down.

Blake was still standing near the boulders, scanning the moonlit prairie, when suddenly Molly Wells emerged from behind a boulder, smiling. Whispering, she said, "Mr. Blake, I hope you will forgive me for eavesdropping, but somehow I knew you were going to talk to Larry about this Spain thing. I had to hear what he said to you."

"I understand, Molly," the tall man replied kindly.

"I just can't let him die, Mr. Blake. I just can't!"

"Well, little lady," he said evenly, "if we get through the battle tomorrow, it looks like your man is going to take on Vic Spain. Spain will kill him."

"I'll tell you what I told Larry tonight, Mr. Blake. I believe in prayer, and I'm asking God to do something that will prevent Larry from having to draw against Vic Spain. My prayers will be answered, Mr. Blake. And Larry won't have to carry any guilt as a coward, either."

Blake grinned and shook his head. "You are some kind of woman, Molly."

Raising up on her toes, Molly planted a kiss on his cheek. "Thank you for trying to help Larry. You're a good man."

As the lovely blonde scurried back to her sleeping place beside her parents, Ross Blake touched the spot on his cheek where she had kissed him. "You are some kind of woman, Molly Wells," he said under his breath. "Some kind of woman."

Chapter Ten

The soft night breeze whispered through the rocks and boulders at the base of Deadman Butte as Ross Blake sat down on a rock. He laid his hat beside him and looked toward the charred remains of the station house, where Walt and Florence Boatman, the stationmaster and his wife, lay dead. He and the others had agreed to bury what was left of their bodies before they pulled out. He had thought a lot of the Boatmans. Sorrow touched him that they should have to die such horrid, violent deaths.

Blake looked at the dark forms of the passengers sleeping on the ground, and he wondered how many of them would die, too, before the encounter with the Sioux was over. A flicker of hope burned within him—hope that by some miracle they would all come through it alive.

His thoughts turned to Molly Wells and Larry Mangrum. *What a tragedy*, he thought. *Those poor kids couldn't have fallen in love at a worse time. Their whole world is sitting on a powder keg . . . and the fuse is lit.* He thought of the love that had danced in Molly's eyes moments ago when she spoke of how much she loved the handsome young cowboy.

Abruptly, Blake thought of Jenny. The familiar hollow feeling that he had known since her death surfaced within im. How empty and void his life was without her! Well-meaning friends had urged him to find another woman, marry, and build a new life, but somehow he could not bring himself to do it. The love between him and his sweet Jenny had been special—very, very special.

Though it brought pain to his heart, Ross Blake let his mind slide back to the day he and Jenny had met. He relived their courtship, their wedding day, the precious years that followed. . . .

Jenny had experienced two miscarriages within the first three years of their marriage, and army doctors told her it would be dangerous to her own life if she tried again to have children. In spite of this, their marriage was blissful, for their love was deep and strong . . . for seven wonderful years.

As Ross Blake sat in the moonlight savoring the priceless recollections of life with Jenny, the black memory of her sudden illness and untimely death rolled through his mind. He was not aware that he was biting down hard until he felt the pain in his jaws.

Shaking his head as if to dispel the bitter memory, Blake told himself that if he did not have the stage line, he would have nothing to live for. And it did not offer much. A grim smile pulled at his lips as he thought, *It's ironic. . . . Life matters so little to me since Jenny died, but tomorrow I'll fight with everything in me to kill Indians and survive. Even a man with little to live for will cling to life with the tenacity of a bulldog.*

At the first hint of dawn, Blake awakened the others and got them ready. He and the other men quickly gathered rocks and buried the charred bodies of the stationmaster and his wife, the imminent battle keeping the men alert and ready to take up their positions. Hunger was gnawing at their stomachs, but all they could do to satiate it was to drink water and concentrate on surviving the coming attack. Betty and Molly, wearing the men's hats, took their positions among the rocks. They had tucked their hair up inside the hats. Ten feet to either side of them were Pete and Larry, their minds steeled against letting the Sioux get near the women.

Marshal Claxton gave water to Jack Parris, who was handcuffed to a doorpost in the stagecoach. It had been moved earlier and was nestled safely behind huge boulders

Parris swore at Claxton and then said, "It's not right to do this to me, Marshal! I'm dead meat if those stinking savages get back in here. You oughtta let me have a gun and—"

"Shut up, Parris!" lashed Claxton. "You've already shown what you would do if you had a gun! You're staying right here just like you are."

Parris's lips lost color as they pressed against his broken teeth. His craggy features revealed his fear. "Claxton!" he said, pleading. "I swear I won't put a gun on you! I just want a chance to defend myself against them dirty red skins! They aren't even human. Come on, give me a chance!"

Claxton moved his face within inches of the pleading man's nose and hissed, "I'm not too sure bounty hunters are human either! You're staying right here in this coach."

With the bounty hunter's vile profanity following him, John Claxton made his way to the spot where he was to defend the ready-made rock fort against the Sioux, about twelve feet from Pete Wells.

Ross Blake and Hal Stacy were stationed an equal distance apart on the other side of Larry Mangrum. Blake had pointed out deep gulches and gullies on the south and west side of their position. These would prevent the Indians from attacking by horseback on those sides. If they were going to ride in, it would have to be on the east side since Deadman Butte protected them on the north. For that reason the stage passengers and crew were tucked in among the rocks, facing east

Blake had also warned them to keep a close watch when the Indians rode in. If the braves left their mounts to attack on foot, they could circle around, climb the rocks, and come in from the south or west. And there were two good reasons not to allow the Indians inside the rock-strewn area. The first was that it would mean hand-to-hand combat, at which the Sioux were experts. The second reason was that if the two women were recognized, the Indians would double their efforts to come in and take Betty and Molly alive.

As the sky lightened, things grew tense. Except for a slight breeze that toyed with the sagebrush and the leaves of scattered trees, the prairie was still.

Larry Mangrum studied the lifeless land for a few moments and then turned to look at Molly. She was obviously frightened, but she afforded him a faint smile. He gave her a reassuring look and said in a low voice, "I love you."

"I love you, too, Larry," she said, also speaking low. "I stayed awake a long time last night praying. Some way, somehow, you won't have to die under Spain's gun. We are going to have our lives together."

Broadening his smile, Larry said, "Molly Wells, they say beauty is only skin deep. But with you it runs all the way through."

Suddenly Ross Blake's voice cut the air. "Heads up, everybody! There they are! Right where we saw them last night."

Outlined against the brightening Wyoming sky were a line of mounted warriors. The first person to complete the count was Hal Stacy. "There are twenty-one now. Two Thumbs must have stayed out of sight when they showed themselves to us yesterday, Ross."

"Could be," agreed Blake.

"I hope that's all there are," spoke up Pete Wells. "If they've got more stashed over that rise, we won't stand a chance."

Blake was about to comment when he saw one rider pull from the line of mounted warriors and begin to pace his horse back and forth in front of them. The horse stood out immediately—it was solid black, while all the others were the normal spotted pintos.

"Notice the black horse?" Blake asked the others.

When they nodded, he said, "That's Two Thumbs. He rides a black stallion with a white star on its face. Can't see the star from here, but you can bet your boots the man on its back is Two Thumbs."

Abruptly the rider on the black horse began riding slowly down the gentle slope of the rise, heading directly toward Deadman Butte. The warriors on the pintos followed, flanking him on both sides.

Blake and the others tensed, knowing the attack would come soon. Death seemed to hover in the cool morning air. The rising sun threw a fan-shaped shaft of light through the low, broken clouds that hovered at the eastern horizon.

Molly turned and gave Larry Mangrum a stronger smile this time. "It's going to be all right, Larry," she said. "We are going to have our life together."

Larry smiled back and then turned to look at the parade of mounted warriors. He let the memory of that reassuring smile linger in his mind. *Molly Wells*, he thought, *I wish I had your faith.*

Two Thumbs halted his black horse about four hundred yards out and watched as his men broke into two groups of seven and one of six. Blake realized that they were going to attack in waves, coming with one group at a time. Two Thumbs, of course, would remain aloof, not taking part in the fight.

The first group of warriors pulled out in front of the others and lined up single file.

"Get ready," said Blake. "Remember what I told you last night. Don't fire until I fire first, and then fire in the order we discussed. That way we won't all be shooting at the same man. We've got to make a dent in their forces quick. The more we kill, the faster they will give up and leave us alone."

Suddenly the lead Indian raised a feathered rifle, shot it angrily above his head, and uttered a wild, animallike cry. The others followed suit as the lead Indian goaded his mount into a full gallop. Each of the stage passengers and crew in the rocks shouldered a rifle and began sighting in on the charging riders. Soon they could hear the thunder of unshod hooves, accompanied by murderous, barbaric cries and doglike yapping.

Within seconds the whooping Indians reached the fringe of where the dead pintos and army bays were scattered about from the previous battle. Coming in single file, they weaved among the dead horses, picking the surest path in a sinuous line. As they drew within forty yards, they started firing toward the rock fortress, where they knew the occupants of the stagecoach were waiting. Sioux bullets whined off the boulders and threw up spurts of dirt in front of them.

Ross Blake drew a bead on the lead Indian and squeezed the trigger of the Winchester. The bronze-bodied man howled as the slug tore into his rib cage, and he peeled off his horse. Suddenly the huge rock pile came alive with the menacing crack of seven Winchesters and the whisper of hot lead.

One of the pintos took a slug in the neck and, screaming wildly, went down nose first. Its rider hit the ground hard, dropping his rifle. Larry Mangrum sighted in on the Indian as he scrambled for his rifle, retrieved it, and dived behind one of the horses that already lay dead on the ground. When he raised his head up to begin shooting, Larry fired. The Indian's head snapped back, and he went down, never to move again.

Two of the Indians fired from their horses at the same time, aiming at the hat worn by Betty Wells. The two bullets whined past her face, causing her to duck down quickly.

Marshal Claxton and Pete Wells fired simultaneously, hitting the same warrior. The man jerked with the impact of two .44 slugs slamming into his body, and he rolled off his horse, dead before he hit the ground.

Blake saw the remaining four braves gallop back to the spot where their friends waited with Two Thumbs, bullets chewing up ground on their heels.

"Hold it!" shouted Blake. "They're getting out of range." Looking around at the others, he asked, "Everybody all right?"

The members of the group assured him they were okay, though Betty was obviously shaken from her close call.

"Reload quick," Blake told them. "The second wave will be on us shortly. Be ready when that one has passed, too, because if they follow Sioux pattern, the third wave will come in without giving us a break." Above the clicking sounds of rifles being reloaded, Blake added, "We got three of them that time. If we can do as well on the next two charges, we just might discourage them. Keep it up."

No sooner had he spoken than the shouts of the second charge met their ears. A cloud of brown dust rose up behind the galloping horses of the seven Sioux, almost hiding Two Thumbs, who remained in the distance.

Hooves thundered and guns roared as the Sioux warriors came in exactly the same pattern as the first wave, weaving in a curved line among the dead horses. Amid the gunfire and increasing clouds of blue-white smoke, lead slugs slammed into the protective rocks above and below Ross Blake and his group, ricocheting with angry whines.

Molly Wells got a charging Indian in her gunsights, followed him briefly, and squeezed off a shot. When the slug hit him, he jerked, threw his rifle in the air, and fell off his pinto. He rolled onto the ground doing somersaults, then lay still.

"Hey, Molly!" shouted Larry Mangrum from his position a few feet away. "That's good shooting!"

Molly turned to grin at him. At the same time, he saw an Indian's rifle, aimed at Molly, blossom with orange flame. The slug chewed into stone next to her face, spraying rock fragments into her eyes. Gasping, she dropped down behind the boulder, blinking and thumbing at her eyes, and as she did, Larry's hat toppled from her head and fell to the ground. Betty dropped down beside her daughter.

Thinking Molly was hit, Larry started to turn toward the women, his heart pounding, but was stopped short when he felt the lashing heat of a bullet snarl past his cheek. He squeezed off another shot at the Indians, who were now fleeing from rifle range, and then moved beside mother and daughter. Pete Wells was also there now, fearful that Molly had been shot.

"She's all right," Betty told them. "She's not hit. Just got some shards of rock in her eyes."

Ross Blake handed Betty a canteen, saying, "Here. Let her wash her eyes with water."

John Claxton and Hal Stacy, who remained at their posts, saw the third wave moving in fast. "Get ready, everybody!" hollered Stacy. "They're coming in fast!"

Larry spoke a few words of comfort to Molly before dashing back to his post. As he picked up her rifle, he thought of the long blond hair that now lay on her shoulders. "Molly!" he called. "When you're able to shoot again, don't forget to put the hat on!"

Molly nodded without looking up. She was busy pouring water into one hand and splashing it into her eyes. "Get back to your position, Mother," she told Betty. "I can do this by myself."

Betty returned to her post, tugging her husband's hat a little tighter on her head.

The third wave was upon them . . . six more warriors, firing their weapons and screeching their war cry. One was shot immediately, falling from his horse to die on the ground. Another had his horse go down under him with a slug in its chest. Amid the smoke and dust, the rider crawled around the south end of the rocks unseen.

Hal Stacy shot a warrior off his pinto just as the third wave was veering off to pull out of range. The Indian was not dead, however, but rose up, firing a shot at the group in the rocks before running away, blood streaming from the wound in his chest. John Claxton aimed at him and fired, hitting him in the back. The man stiffened, dropped his rifle, clawed for the sky, and fell facedown.

The third wave was barely over when the Sioux who had come in the first wave were charging in again. The staccato sound of gunfire came from the rocks once more as the attacking riders followed the same pattern, weaving among the dead horses and blasting away.

Pete Wells opened fire, but on the second pull of the trigger he heard the hollow sound of the hammer striking an empty chamber. Dropping down out of the line of fire, he opened the chamber and began reloading from a box of cartridges. At the same moment, he spotted movement among the jumbled rocks to the west. A Sioux warrior, dressed in only a breechclout, had dropped from a boulder and was running toward Marshal John Claxton, wielding a long-bladed knife. Claxton, busy firing at the present charge, was apparently unaware of the Indian's presence.

Pete Wells dropped his rifle, its chamber still open, and headed for the Indian. The brave saw him coming but continued to bring down the knife at Claxton's back. The threat of Wells's attack threw the Indian off balance as he brought down the knife, and it went into the marshal's left shoulder rather than the center of his back.

Claxton went down with the knife buried in his flesh as Wells hit the warrior with a flying tackle. Both weaponless, the two men began swinging fists. At one point in the scuffle, the Indian's line of sight fell on Molly, whose long blond hair had not yet been concealed again by the hat, and Wells saw the surprised look in the Indian's eyes.

The red man connected solidly with Wells's jaw, staggering him. With his opponent off balance, the Indian wheeled and ran toward the boulders where he had come in. Just as he reached the boulders and began to climb over one of them, Wells caught him by the ankles and pulled him down to his knees. Again the Sioux knocked Wells off balance, this time by swinging his elbow around fast, striking Wells in the jaw. While Wells regained his footing, the Indian once more ran for the boulder. The area was rocking with gunfire as the attack continued.

Pete Wells dashed up behind the fleeing Indian and sank his fingers into his coal-black hair. Using the Indian's momentum, Wells rammed his face into the side of the boulder. The Indian groaned and tried to fight back, but Wells still had a solid grip on his hair. Gritting his teeth, he slammed the Indian's face into the boulder repeatedly, and blood spurted from the man's nose and mouth, making a shiny red smear on the hard rock.

Like a wild man, Wells continued ramming the Indian's head into the rock even after the man went limp and died. Finally, when his arms lost their strength, he let the dead Indian fall to the ground. Panting for air, he dashed to the fallen lawman and found him conscious. Claxton was lying facedown, trying to reach the embedded knife with his right hand.

"Here, Marshal," gasped Wells, "I'll pull it out. Brace yourself."

Claxton passed out then, and at the same moment, Ross Blake put a bullet into the heart of another of the Sioux. As the brave toppled from his horse, the two remaining Indians galloped away, returning to their chief.

Blake was aware that Marshal Claxton was down. When the firing stopped, he called to his shotgunner, "Hal, keep your eyes on the Indians. Holler if they start another charge."

Hal Stacy nodded and turned his eyes toward the gathering of Sioux on the plain while the others hurried to the spot where the wounded lawman lay on the ground. Betty knelt beside him and examined the wound. Looking up at Blake, she said, "The knife went pretty deep. He's bleeding profusely. We'll have to cauterize the wound to stop it."

Pete Wells immediately began gathering brush for a fire, intending to heat the blade of the Indian's knife to do the cauterizing. While the blade was being heated and the marshal's shirt was being removed, Ross Blake looked toward Hal Stacy and asked what the Indians were doing.

"I think they're licking their wounds," came Stacy's reply. "We killed eight of them. There's only thirteen left, including Two Thumbs. They've dismounted. I don't think they'll be back for a while."

"Watch them close and keep me posted," said Blake.

"Will do." Stacy nodded.

Within ten minutes the unconscious lawman's wound was cauterized, and the bleeding had stopped. Betty bathed his face with water for several minutes, and finally he began to awaken. Shortly he was fully conscious and feeling the pain of his wound. Molly, who was able to see again, explained to him how her father had saved his life by charging the Indian unarmed. He had killed the warrior with his bare hands, she said.

Gritting his teeth against the pain, Claxton set his firm gaze on Wells and said, "I want to thank you for what you did, Pete. If that knife had gone in where the Indian no doubt was aiming it, I'd be a dead man."

Betty smiled and said, "See, Marshal, I told you Pete is a different man."

Chapter Eleven

Belly-down on top of a hill to the northeast, Max Lund and the dozen men he had brought with him from the Hole-in-the-Wall were watching the Indian attacks on the white people in the rocks at the base of Deadman Butte. From their position, Lund and his men could see the metal rack on top of the stagecoach, hidden among the boulders.

The muscular German swore and said, "I sure hope Jack Parris is still alive. I would hate for those Indians to kill him when I want the pleasure for myself."

Hugh Milner, one of Lund's outlaw friends, said, "Looks pretty good for the whites so far, Max. They've been pickin' them redskins off right and left."

"Yeah," spoke up one named Russ Wyatt. "Somebody in that bunch is plenty good with a rifle."

"All I can do is wait and keep hopin'," said Lund. "One thing we ain't gonna do is take on those Sioux. If the whites survive and head on for Rawlins, we'll move in and capture Parris. That bounty hunter is gonna wish he'd never been born."

As the morning wore on, the twelve warriors and their chief remained out of rifle range. They were sitting in a

151

circle on the ground, apparently carrying on a serious conversation.

While Hal Stacy waited and watched from atop a small rock, the others from the stagecoach sat on the ground near the spot where Marshal Claxton lay. He was in a great deal of pain but was suffering quietly for the sake of the others. Jack Parris, however, was bellowing from the stagecoach for someone to come to him. He was being ignored.

Larry Mangrum looked at the ex-cavalry officer and said, "What do you think Two Thumbs is planning, Mr. Blake?"

"Hard to say," came Blake's reply. "By virtue of the fact they are still out there in plain sight, I can assure you he's not through with us. I'm just mighty thankful Pete killed that Sioux who got in here. Two Thumbs still doesn't know we have women with us."

Betty sat next to Pete and patted his arm. "He's my hero," she said proudly.

Marshal Claxton surprised everybody by saying, "He's mine, too, ma'am."

Pete Wells looked at the lawman and grinned.

"Two Thumbs will no doubt come at us again," Blake said to the group. "The question is when. He's smart enough to know that we weren't carrying a lot of food on the stage, and he knows everything in the station was burned. He and his men can live on small game, but we would have to expose ourselves to go hunting. We can still get water from the well behind the station, but we're going to need food pretty soon, or we're in trouble—and that black-eyed savage knows it. He might just lay in for a siege and try to starve us out."

"The way my stomach feels," said Hal Stacy from his perch, "that isn't going to take much longer."

"Don't worry," said Blake, looking up at him. "We're going to eat tonight."

"You know of a café nearby?" asked Stacy, grinning down at his boss.

"No, but we're having meat and potatoes . . . without the potatoes. We dropped two pintos out there today. Their meat will be fresh enough to eat tonight."

"I've never had horsemeat before," put in Molly, "but right now I think I could even eat rattlesnake meat."

"Cooked, of course," Pete said, grinning. Molly smiled at him.

"Keep a good lookout," John Claxton said from his prone position. "I've never known of an Indian to be as vicious as Two Thumbs."

Molly turned her face toward the lawman and asked, "Marshal, why is Two Thumbs so much more vengeful than other Sioux warriors?"

Swinging his eyes toward the stage-line owner, he said, "Why don't you tell her about it, Blake?"

Ross Blake saw the curiosity on the faces of every person in the group. "None of you know?" he asked.

They all shook their heads.

Blake looked up to his shotgunner on the rock. "Any change, Hal?"

"Nope," came the reply. "They're just sitting there talking."

Blake nodded, then brought his attention to the people around him. "The vengeance Two Thumbs harbors," he told them, "has to do with his name."

"His name?" said Molly. "It is an odd one, but then so are many of the names the Indians give their children."

"His parents did not give him that name," said Blake. "They gave him the name Angry Wolf." Blake proceeded to tell his listeners the full story of Angry Wolf's prowess in hand-to-hand combat, of his capture and maiming by the cavalry unit, and of his subsequent torture and massacre of the same unit.

There was a quizzical look in Larry Mangrum's eyes as Ross Blake finished the story. "I don't understand, Mr.

Blake. You just told us that the greatest shame that can come on a Sioux warrior is for him to be maimed so he can no longer do battle."

"That's right. To their minds that is the greatest ignominy that can befall a man of war. It leaves him without honor, sort of like a second-class citizen."

"But his people don't treat him as if he were shamed," reasoned Larry. "He's still chief."

"There's a reason for that," said Blake. "As Angry Wolf, he had built up such a reputation for himself that the Hunkpapas already considered him some kind of a god. That's the stature he has with them today. But he can no longer fight the way he used to, and his vengeance toward whites is like a seething volcano. He is especially merciless toward white women, because they bear white boys who grow up to become soldiers. They are always brutally raped before he starts his torture, but the excruciating torment and agony he puts them through before they finally die beggars mortal description."

No one in the group said much after that, and the morning passed into afternoon and early evening with the Sioux remaining at the same spot. Just before the last light of the day disappeared, the Indians rose in plain view, loading their guns. Ross Blake watched the open display and then turned to his friends and said, "That's their way of telling us they'll be attacking in the morning."

Larry Mangrum asked, "Mr. Blake, is it possible that Two Thumbs has more warriors but hasn't shown them?"

"It's definitely possible," replied Blake. "He's a sneaky one, I'll tell you."

"But what do you think?"

"I think we're looking at all he has within reasonable distance. If he had more, he probably would have already thrown them at us. But on the other hand he could be playing with us. The Sioux love these waiting games. They like to drive their enemies mad."

"If he has more warriors stashed close, we've had it."

"That's about it," said Blake soberly. "But if they come back with the twelve they have left out there, I have a plan that just might wipe out enough of them to send Two Thumbs and the others running."

All eyes were fastened on Blake in the dying light. He looked toward the Indians and saw that they were riding south. When they disappeared in the gathering gloom, he turned to his curious group and said, "My plan is to adopt an old Indian trick and use it against them." Having their full attention, he went on to explain how the Sioux sometimes buried themselves in shallow spots, covering themselves with a layer of dirt and brush. Then they would rise up from their hiding places just as their enemies drew near, shooting them down before they knew what happened. "If we work things just right," he concluded, "we can take them by surprise and turn the tables on them."

Before the moon came up, Blake took Stacy, Larry, and Wells with him. He led them out in the field where the dead horses lay, pointing out that every time the Indians attacked, they had taken the same winding path. "We'll dig out four places," he said, gesturing in the near dark. "Two on each side of the approach. When they send in the first wave of six, we'll spring up with them between us and catch them in a crossfire."

"Are you sure they won't send all twelve at us at once?" asked Wells.

"It's unlikely," commented Blake. "My guess is that he'll divide what he has left into two groups and hit us with waves as before."

"Unless he's fooled us and has more warriors," put in Hal Stacy.

"If he does, we're done for anyhow, Hal," said Blake. "We're going to have to gamble on it, but if I'm right, this trick will get us out of here alive. We'll have to kill all the Indians in the first wave and then dash back into the rocks before the second wave can come. Losing that many at once may discourage the remaining Indians enough to send them away licking their wounds."

The four men scooped out places in which to hide themselves the next morning. Then they cut up the hindquarters of a pinto and carried the meat back to where the women waited with the wounded marshal. A fire was built, and the meat was roasted. Ross Blake carried meat and water to the sullen bounty hunter. Everyone ate heartily, glad for the nourishment, and almost immediately they began to feel their strength returning. After the meal, Pete and Betty sat down near the marshal, while Larry and Molly strolled toward the south side of the rock pile by the light of the moon.

Finding a place just out of sight of the others, the young couple embraced, kissed, and then clung to each other. With Molly's head lying against his chest, Larry held her tight and said, "Well, darling, we made it through one day."

"Thank heaven," she said.

"I already have," he breathed, smiling. "I can almost believe that we're going to make it out of here alive. Mr. Blake is a mighty smart man. His idea to use the Indians' own trick on them just might work. It's the Vic Spain situation that bothers me."

Molly pulled her head back so she could look him in the eye. "That's going to work out, too. I just know it."

Shaking his head, Larry said, "I sure wish I had the same confidence you have."

The couple kissed again and then returned to the others.

Blake said to the group, "Time for bed, everybody. More fighting to do tomorrow. You need your rest."

"So do you," said Larry Mangrum. "Did you sleep at all last night?"

"Uh . . . not much."

"Not *any*, you mean. You were sort of keeping watch, weren't you?"

Blake grinned. "Well, I just thought it best if one of us kept an eye on things."

"Fine," said Larry. "You get some sleep, and tonight I'll keep an eye on things."

Blake agreed, and everyone made preparations for sleeping. As Larry climbed up on a tall rock to keep watch, the rest of them bedded down.

Molly was just about to stretch out near her parents, when her mother took her elbow and said quietly, "Come over here for a minute, dear. I want to talk to you." Betty led Molly out of hearing range of the men and said, "Molly, I want you to know that I really like Larry. I hope it turns out all right for the two of you. Your father likes him very much, too."

Smiling, Molly hugged her mother and said, "I'm glad you both like him."

"Has he told you in so many words that he loves you?"

Molly sighed. "He sure has."

"Good," breathed Betty. "I only wish he would give up the idea of facing Vic Spain."

"It's going to be all right, Mother," said Molly. "I just know it."

Dawn was no more than a hint on the eastern horizon when the stagecoach group breakfasted on cold horsemeat that had been cooked the night before. While they ate, Ross Blake went over his plan with the three men and the two women. Just before sunup, Blake, Wells, Stacy, and Larry would lie down in the scooped-out places they had prepared the night before, and the two women would cover them with dirt and brush. The men would rely on Betty and Molly to start shooting at the precise instant the attacking warriors were in position for the surprise crossfire. Their shots would be the signal for the men to rise up and cut down the hostiles. Betty was to alert them when the first charge started, and call out how many were coming before the Indians were in hearing range.

Jack Parris, still tied to the coach, was given food and water by Larry Mangrum. His mood was more sour than ever. When the young cowboy walked away without saying anything, Parris swore vehemently at him.

Marshal Claxton was braced up against a boulder and given a rifle. If the Indians were to get inside the rock enclosure, at least he would be in a position to defend himself.

Minutes before the light of the rising sun was bright enough to allow the Indians to see what they were doing, the four men lay facedown in the shallow holes with their guns beneath them. The two women then covered them with dirt and brush, leaving holes for them to breathe, before taking their places among the boulders, wearing the men's hats as usual.

Soon the fiery rim of the sun appeared on the earth's eastern edge. For a few moments the Wyoming prairie took on a yellow-orange hue, and Deadman Butte came alive with color, starting at the top and slowly working its way down.

The four men waited in the darkness of their graves, breathing through the small openings left by the women. Abruptly they heard Betty call out, "The Sioux are in sight! There are still only thirteen of them!"

Blake, Wells, Stacy, and Larry were glad to hear that the number had not increased. Nerves tense, they waited quietly for Betty to tell them that the first charge was coming.

Suddenly, from her place in the rocks, Betty Wells called out, "Here they come! There are six of them in this wave!"

Betty and her daughter laid their rifles on top of the rock and made ready. "We can only shoot once, Molly," said Betty. "After that, the men will be up. So make your first shot count."

Molly nodded, thinking of Larry out there under the dirt. Whispering a prayer, she braced herself.

At that instant the rumble of thundering hooves blended with the Sioux war cry, penetrating the early morning air. The four men in the shallow holes could feel the sudden trembling of the earth. Lying there under the thin layer of dirt and brush, each one tensed, waiting for the women to signal. Before long the charging warriors seemed to be right on top of them, but the men waited as the thunder of the hooves and the high-pitched whoops grew louder and louder.

Betty and Molly were sighting in on the lead Indian as the galloping riders entered the area strewn with dead horses and began the same pattern, weaving among them. Betty licked her lips and cried, "Now, Molly!" Both women squeezed the triggers.

Before the Indians could unleash a volley of shots, they were stunned by the four figures that rose up like brown ghosts from the earth, rifles blazing. The lead Indian, hit by the two bullets fired by the women, reeled off his pinto and hit the ground. The next four riders took hot slugs as Blake, Wells, Stacy and Larry fired at them point-blank. The frightened Indian ponies, their riders no longer on their backs, kept on running.

The sixth Sioux had only a brief moment to react before the white men could work the levers of their rifles and cut him down. Just before they shot him, he fired at Hal Stacy. The redheaded shotgunner took the bullet in the right shoulder, the impact spinning him around before he dropped to the ground, the rifle falling from his hand. Seconds later the Indian who had shot Stacy was dead from the barrage of bullets.

At that instant, the three other men saw one of the fallen Indians rise up, bringing his gun to bear. All three of them shot him, and he flopped backward, dead. While this was happening, Stacy was rising to his feet, holding his wounded shoulder. He was glassy-eyed, obviously in a state of shock. Blood poured through his fingers onto the thirsty ground below as he stumbled blindly toward the place where the lead Indian had fallen. No one was aware that the Indian was still alive.

The three men started for Stacy, eager to help him. Suddenly the lead Indian rose to his knees, blood flowing from the two bullet holes in his upper body. Bringing up his rifle, he fired at Stacy, hitting him in the heart. Immediately afterward three guns roared, and the Indian fell dead. Blake dashed to Stacy, took one look, and told the others he was gone. All three men turned toward the Sioux out on the prairie.

Ross Blake handed his rifle to Larry Mangrum and hoisted Hal Stacy's lifeless body over his shoulder. They quickly made their way back into the rock enclosure. The women were saddened at Stacy's death, as was John Claxton. The body was placed out of sight for burial later, and everyone's attention returned to the seven Indians out on the prairie. In the distance, they could see Two Thumbs waving his arms wildly, as though ranting and raving in a frenzy.

"I think we made him angry," Larry said as Molly was brushing dirt from his back and from his hair. Betty was doing the same for Pete.

"Yeah." Blake nodded. "He'll send the rest of them at us shortly. You can count on it. We can't use the trick a second time, but I have another plan."

All eyes turned to Blake, waiting for him to tell his plan. "I mentioned earlier that Two Thumbs has become something of a god to the Sioux. If I could sneak out and capture him during the next attack, it just might take the spirit out of the others—especially if I threaten to kill their god. We could take Two Thumbs all the way to Rawlins with us as a safety measure."

The group agreed that it was worth a try. Blake reminded them to be very careful when the six Indians attacked. When the braves realized there were only four people shooting at them, they might rush in to fight hand-to-hand. If that happened, it would be all over quickly. Claxton was out of commission, and the two women could not fight vicious, well-trained Sioux warriors. Wells and Larry would be hopelessly outnumbered.

Moments later, armed to the teeth with bows as well as rifles, the six Sioux warriors galloped toward Deadman Butte. When Blake and his friends saw them coming, Blake went over the rocks to the west as the others took up their battle stations. This time the Sioux surprised the stagecoach group by diving from their mounts, each warrior then taking refuge behind a dead horse. Guns boomed from both sides, but Indians and whites were well protected, and no one was getting hit.

While the gunfight went on, Ross Blake made his way to where Two Thumbs sat his black stallion, observing the battle. Blake kept to the gullies as he ran southward in a wide circle, drawing up about twenty feet behind the infamous chief. He could hear the crackle of gunfire as, hunkering low in a shallow gully, he caught his breath. Then he made ready to act.

Looking up at Two Thumbs silhouetted against the blue sky, Blake could not help but admire him. He sat on his horse with his back absolutely straight, wearing a full feathered headdress from which fell a shower of long black hair, glistening over his broad shoulders. His back and arms rippled with muscles. His only physical flaws were the two mangled hands, with scarred stumps where the thumbs used to be.

Slowly, Blake climbed from the gully, bending low with his revolver in his right hand. Just as he sprang forward, the black horse nickered, and the chief whipped around. But he was too late. Blake's revolver came down on his head with a sodden sound, and Two Thumbs fell to the ground, unconscious.

Less than ten minutes later, Blake, sitting behind Two Thumbs on the Indian's horse, rode to where the Sioux warriors were now lobbing arrows into the rocks from their places behind the dead horses. When they heard Blake's voice thunder at them, the Indians stopped, turning to stare with amazement at the white man mounted on the black horse with Two Thumbs in front of him, the muzzle of Blake's cocked revolver held in the groggy chief's mouth.

Removing the revolver from Two Thumbs's mouth, Blake commanded the chief to tell his warriors to lay down their weapons and stand up. When the dazed man gave them the order in the Sioux tongue, they obeyed, their eyes wide, fearful of what might happen to their vulnerable god.

With a threatening tone in his voice, Blake then said to the chief, "Tell your men that I will set you free when we get near Rawlins—but only if I do not see the hair of a Sioux on the rest of the trip. If I so much as see the shadow of a Sioux, I will kill you. Understand?"

Two Thumbs nodded, and he quickly told his men what Blake had said. The six warriors looked at their leader with trepidation. Then they began moving away, searching for their scattered horses so they could ride. Minutes later they were galloping west together, and soon they were out of sight.

Once Two Thumbs was securely handcuffed to the doorpost of the stagecoach opposite Jack Parris, Hal Stacy was given a quick burial. The black stallion belonging to Two Thumbs was tied to the rear of the vehicle. With Hal Stacy's revolver on his hip, Pete Wells sat between the Indian and the bounty hunter. Across from Wells sat the wounded marshal and the two women.

The stage rocked as Larry Mangrum and Ross Blake climbed up into the box. The owner of the stage line released the brake and nudged the team forward, the black stallion behind trotting along as the harness rattled and the wheels squeaked.

The stage rolled southward toward the open prairie, away from Deadman Butte and the jumble of boulders that had shielded the travelers so well.

Molly Wells took one look back and then glanced skyward. *Thank you,* she silently breathed.

Chapter Twelve

From their hiding place on the hilltop, Max Lund and his men watched the scene at the base of Deadman Butte with interest as the Indian chief was taken hostage. Not long after the six warriors had ridden away, leaving their chief in the hands of the whites, the stagecoach was pulled into the open, the Indian hostage being placed inside it as the rest of the passengers and crew prepared to leave.

Lund's eyes widened when he saw Jack Parris released from the stagecoach and allowed to walk around. Grinning with wicked delight, the big German said, "Our boy Jack is still alive! I'm gonna have my fun with him after all!"

"Let's go, Max," one of the outlaws said. "We can take that stage anytime now."

"Not so fast, Frank." Lund lifted a hand in restraint. "Them redskins that rode away may have plans to jump the stage and retrieve their friend. I don't want to tangle with 'em. Let's follow the stage at a distance and make sure those Indians ain't around before we move in and take Parris."

Eager to be on the move, the outlaws mounted up and rode slowly down the hill, out of sight of the stage, which was just pulling out as the men reached level ground. They followed far enough behind so as not to be noticed from the stagecoach or by any Indians that might be lingering near it. Before they realized it, the stage was pulling into the small town of Arminto.

Lund swore, saying they would just have to wait until the stage left the town. He did not want a bunch of townspeople gawking when he and his men took Parris off the stage.

It was late morning when Ross Blake guided the stage onto Arminto's main street. He and Larry Mangrum gasped at the horrendous sight that lay before them. Naked bloody bodies of men, women, and children were strewn along the main street and side streets, scattered on boardwalks, lying in doorways and on the porches of houses. The entire population of Arminto appeared to have been massacred, scalped, and mutilated. The Sioux had already been there. Blake decided that Two Thumbs must have had a larger force than the one at Deadman Butte when he did this.

As Blake kept the stage moving slowly up the street, he could hear gagging sounds and sobs coming from inside the coach. Reaching the center of town, he halted the team and climbed down from the box. Stepping to the window where Two Thumbs was shackled to the doorpost, he said, "You did this, didn't you?"

The Indian glared at him with cold, black eyes, holding his mouth rigid, his silence answer enough.

Blake's features hardened. "These people were almost totally unarmed, Two Thumbs," he said through clenched teeth. "Some brave warrior you are! You even make war on women and helpless little children."

Pursing his lips, the stone-faced chief spit in Blake's face.

Blake, reacting instinctively, raised a fist and drew it back, but before he brought it to bear on Two Thumbs he caught himself. Eyes blazing, he wiped away the spittle.

"Let me loose, Blake!" shouted Jack Parris, glaring at the Indian. "Let me loose, and I'll tear him apart—dirty, stinking, inhuman beast!"

Two Thumbs regarded the bounty hunter with an impassive stare.

Blake said to the other occupants of the stage, "No telling how many more hostile Sioux are in this area. I think it would be best for us to head over to Casper, even though we have Two Thumbs. An army camp often sets up just outside of town. If they aren't there, we can go on into Casper and wire Fort Fetterman for help in getting on to Rawlins."

"Casper's about sixty miles, isn't it?" asked Pete Wells.

"Right. It's almost twice that far to Rawlins." Blake looked around the town and then continued, "I think the best thing is for us to feed the horses at one of the barns here and fix a meal for ourselves at one of the houses. I know the idea of food isn't too appealing right now, but we've got to eat if we want to keep up our strength. Then we'll push on to Casper."

The others agreed. They quickly found a barn with plenty of grain and hay for the team. The house in front of it was empty, its occupants apparently having been elsewhere when the killing started. Betty and Molly took up the task of cooking a meal from the well-stocked pantry while Blake, Larry, and Wells carried the wounded marshal inside the house and then took the horses to the barn for feeding.

The meal was almost ready when the men returned to release Parris and the Indian from the coach. Inside the house, Marshal Claxton sat near the table in an overstuffed chair, insisting he could feed himself with his good arm. The bounty hunter and Two Thumbs had their hands cuffed in front of them, enabling them to eat, and were sitting beside each other at the table. Larry Mangrum was sitting on the other side of Two Thumbs, while Blake and

Wells sat across from them. The two women sat at the ends of the table.

Although it was a treat for the beleaguered passengers and crew of the stagecoach to have normal food again, they found it difficult to enjoy their meal in the midst of such carnage. Talk was minimal as they took in what nourishment they could.

While Jack Parris clumsily ate with his hands cuffed, he noticed that Two Thumbs was not eating. Parris resented having to sit next to the Indian, but he knew it would have done him no good to insist on sitting elsewhere, so he had not argued about it. Awkwardly cutting a piece of meat with a table knife, he turned to the Indian and snarled, "Hey, redskin! You too good to eat with white folks?"

Two Thumbs fixed him with an icy glare.

Parris gripped the knife solidly with both hands and ran his furtive gaze over the others. No one was looking at him at the moment, not even Two Thumbs. Twisting on his chair, Parris suddenly raised up the knife and rammed the blade into the Indian's throat.

Two Thumbs jerked from the impact, tipping his chair over backward and falling to the floor, the blade buried in his throat with blood spurting from around it. A gurgling, gagging sound came from the Indian's throat as he attempted to get a grip on the handle with his thumbless hands.

Ross Blake, who had been lifting a cup of steaming coffee to his lips when the knife went into the Indian's throat, impulsively threw the coffee into the bounty hunter's face, causing Parris to howl, flinging his hands up. Larry Mangrum dropped to the floor and yanked the knife from the Indian's throat as Blake rounded the table and smashed a pistonlike punch to the bounty hunter's jaw, knocking him across the room. Bouncing off the wall, Parris dropped to the floor, out cold.

When Parris came to, he was in the stagecoach, shackled once again to the doorpost. The two women were tending to Two Thumbs, who was sagging in one corner of the coach's compartment. They had the Indian's throat packed with cloth, but it was soaked with blood. Marshal Claxton was seated next to Parris. Two Thumbs's black stallion had been fed and watered with the team and was once again tied to the rear of the coach.

Larry Mangrum was already in the box, and Ross Blake was about to climb up when he saw that Parris was awake. Halting at the window, he said, "With an act like that, you're no less a savage than Two Thumbs, Parris."

The bounty hunter's temper erupted, and a wildness showed on his scalded face as he hissed, "You ought to thank me, Blake! That stinking beast won't bother you anymore! I hope he dies!"

Blake looked past Parris to Betty Wells, who was tending to the Indian. "How is he, Betty?"

The unmistakable pallor of death was on the Indian's leathery face. "I don't think he's going to make it, Ross," she answered grimly. "He's losing blood fast."

"Well, hold on, everybody," Blake said as he turned to mount the coach. "The horses are full of oats and ready for a run. We're going to Casper like the devil was after us!"

The Concord rolled southeast out of Arminto, surging and swaying over the weatherworn ruts leading to Casper. Larry Mangrum ran his gaze over the land in search of Indians as the coach picked up speed, the black horse still following behind.

The stage was passing through a rocky area some four miles east of Arminto when Betty Wells called up to the box, asking Ross Blake to stop. As the dust was being carried away by the afternoon breeze, Blake's feet touched ground. Looking through the window at him, Betty said, "Two Thumbs is dead."

Blake threw a steamy look at Jack Parris, then said, "We'd best bury him right here."

Blake, Larry, and Wells made a hasty burial of the Indian, covering him with rocks at the base of a huge boulder. As they were throwing the last few rocks on the pile, a dozen rough-looking men came around the boulder, fronted by a big blond man. Their guns were drawn and cocked.

Larry stiffened, lowering his hand toward his revolver.

"Forget it, kid," Blake said hastily.

"He's right, kid." Max Lund grinned. "You'll just be so much coyote meat if you touch that weapon."

"There isn't any money on this stage," Ross Blake said levelly.

"We ain't after money, mister," retorted Lund. "At least not this time. All we want is that snivelin' bounty hunter you got in the coach."

At that moment Jack Parris recognized Max Lund's deep voice, and sticking his head out the window, he half screamed with panic, "Blake! You can't let him take me! Please, Blake!"

Ross Blake turned and eyed Parris without expression. "You want me to take on this army?" he asked blandly.

"That's bein' smart, mister driver," said Lund. "Just take the cuffs off the slimy snake and we'll be on our way. We won't bother you nor them pretty gals if you do as I say."

A faint sheen of sweat was on the bounty hunter's hollow cheeks as Ross Blake removed the handcuffs at gunpoint. Eyes bulging with fear, Parris said hoarsely, "Please, Blake. You've got to do something! These men will kill me!"

"You can grovel later, Parris," Lund grunted. "Shut your trap for now."

Blake and the others watched as the outlaws untied the black stallion from the rear of the stagecoach and hoisted Jack Parris, frightened and weak kneed, onto its back. Parris was pleading for help as he was led away by the column of riders heading north toward the Hole-in-the-Wall.

* * *

An hour later, Max Lund and his friends moved northward in an uneven column with a terrified Jack Parris riding beside Lund on the black stallion. Parris had wept the whole time. Weary of it, Lund snapped at him, "You shut your trap right now, bounty hunter, or I'm gonna cut your tongue out! I'm lettin' you live till we get to the Hole. Now be thankful for that!"

His face pinched in fear, Parris stopped weeping. But moments later, he let out a scream. Instantly his captors saw what had caused it—a band of Sioux on war-painted pintos was thundering in on them from the west.

"Don't panic!" Lund said to the others, signaling for the column to halt. "There must be two dozen of 'em, and we can't outrun their horses. They're not bringin' their guns to bear. Maybe they only want to talk to us. Let me handle it, okay?"

The warriors, led by a tall Indian wearing war paint, drew up and surrounded the riders. The leader moved to the black stallion, and when he noticed the star on its face, his dark eyes turned to Jack Parris, flashing with contempt. "White-eyes thief steal Two Thumbs' horse!" he blared in broken English.

Parris froze. Max Lund cleared his throat and said, "This man is an outlaw, Chief. We're a posse from up in Buffalo. Now, we can let you have the horse, but the man has to pay his dues to us. You understand?"

"He's lyin'!" Parris shrieked, hoping he had found a way out of his predicament. "I'm a lawman, see, and these men are outlaws. I put this big one here in jail once, and now he's going to kill me for it. Please, take me with you. I'll see that you are given a big reward for saving my life."

The Indian eyed him coldly. "You have badge?"

"Uh . . . no, Chief," gasped Parris. "These . . . these guys took it from me and threw it away."

Max Lund started to speak, but the Indian threw up his hand and grunted, "No more white-eyes lies! Warriors looking for Two Thumbs now. They be here soon. We wait."

The circle of dark-skinned Indians raised their rifles, making the outlaws look down twenty-five black, threatening bores as they were disarmed and forced to leave their saddles. The Indian leader sat them on the ground and made them wait silently while he watched the south for the appearance of the other Sioux warriors.

Just over an hour had passed when a cloud of dust was seen due south. Within minutes it was evident that the other half of the war party was coming at a gallop. The outlaws looked at each other with fear on their faces. If the other group of Sioux had found their dead chief, things could get sticky. Jack Parris was glad that no one here knew he was the one who had put the knife in Two Thumbs's throat.

The newly arrived party of warriors thundered to a halt. Parris watched with trepidation as the chief of the party dismounted and walked over to the leader of the group holding them. The two men talked briefly, and then Parris saw the tall Indian's face grow red as if with anger as he turned toward Max Lund and the others. Shouting something to his men, the Indian stomped toward the outlaws and the bounty hunter, who by now was quivering in his boots.

"Two Thumbs' body found buried in rocks with hole in his neck! You, white-eyes, have Two Thumbs' horse! You killed Two Thumbs!" He turned toward the warriors and, raising his fist high, shouted, "White eyes will die!"

While Parris and the outlaws begged for their lives, the Indian stepped apart from the crowd, ignoring them. He and the leader of the other Sioux party discussed something between themselves and then gave the command for the outlaws to mount up. Jack Parris was made to ride double with Max Lund, and the black stallion was led riderless as the Indians took their prisoners northwest. It was obvious to Parris that the Indians were well acquainted with the territory and knew exactly where they were going.

Parris was certain that the Indians were going to kill him and the outlaws. Not only did he fear death itself, but also the way it was going to come. This ride had purpose behind it; the Indian had something special in mind for the men who had murdered his god.

Jack Parris cursed himself for his greed. If he had not been after the five thousand dollars, he would not be in this fix now.

The ride ended in thirty minutes at a dry, barren area dotted with anthills. Jack Parris's eyes bulged when he saw them. They were alive with millions of scurrying red ants. His chest felt cold and constricted, and his heart pounded furiously. The others were just as frightened. Again he begged for mercy.

The trembling prisoners dismounted and stood in a cluster. The Indian stood facing them, his black eyes vengeful, his voice harsh. "White murderers killed Two Thumbs! Now you pay!"

The captives broke into a babble of frenzied denials, but the leader of the Sioux party paid them no mind. Instead, he commanded his warriors to strip the white men naked, tie their bound wrists to their ankles, and throw them on the anthills.

Screaming in protest, Parris and the outlaws were stripped of their clothing. First their wrists were tied together behind them with short lengths of the sturdy coils of rope that hung from several saddles, and then their ankles were bound. Each naked man was pushed forward onto his knees, and his wrists were tied to his ankles behind him, preventing him from even rising to his feet. Thus bound, the captives were heaved by strong hands onto the mounds that swarmed with red ants. With looks of satisfaction on their faces, the Indians formed a circle around the anthills, ready to kick any of the tied-up men who tried to roll away from the biting red insects.

Jack Parris and the other men writhed in agony as their bodies stung with pain from the ants. With their hands tied, the men were helpless, unable to brush the insects away or otherwise protect themselves. Parris wailed unabashedly—but the next thing he saw turned his blood to ice.

The Indians must have known of a rattlesnake nest nearby, because several were approaching the captives, carrying hissing diamondbacks with long sticks. As soon as the Indians reached the naked men, they threw the snakes among them, and the snakes began to strike furiously at the writhing figures that seemed to threaten them.

In blind anguish, Jack Parris, his body covered with ants, tried to roll away from the snakes. Immediately a diamondback closed in on him, imbedding its poison fangs in his body. Screaming at the top of his lungs, the bounty-hunter could do nothing but watch as a second snake approached, coiled, and then struck. Within minutes, Parris was unconscious and well on his way to breathing his last.

Little by little the bedlam subsided as the other men began to die. To the Sioux, who had lost their god, revenge was sweet.

Arriving in Casper, Ross Blake went to the army camp just outside of town to report the massacre of the cavalry unit at Deadman Butte. The officer in charge already knew about it. He explained that a rider from the platoon that was escorting the northbound stagecoach from Rawlins to Deadman Butte had come in only moments earlier. The coach's crew and their escorts had found the dead horses and the graves. The rider had been dispatched by the lieutenant in charge to bring the news, saying that the platoon was going to stay with the stage all the way to Buffalo. Blake was happy to learn this.

The commander gave Blake a new unit to escort the coach, and within an hour they were on their way southwest. At the end of the second day, they drew near Rawlins.

Darkness was falling, and the platoon bid them good night, saying they would camp outside of town. Just outside the city limits, Ross Blake stopped the stagecoach. Climbing down from the box, he leaned into the window next to where Larry Mangrum was seated beside Molly Wells and said, "Larry, here's your chance to change your mind. Get out now. Let me go into town and—"

"We've already been over this, Mr. Blake," Larry replied dolefully. "I must do what I have to do."

Molly's entire body was shaking. With tears brimming in her eyes, she gripped Larry's arms and begged, "Please, Larry. We got here safely when we could have died at Deadman Butte. Don't rush things. Let there be time for my prayers to be answered."

Larry took her into his arms. "There isn't time, Molly," he said, his voice quavering. "If this stagecoach shows up in Rawlins and I'm not on it, my parents and others will become victims of Vic Spain's malevolence. I can't let that happen."

Molly burst into tears, pressing her face against Larry's chest.

As the young woman cried, the other passengers sat quietly. During the tense moment, the wounded marshal said to Pete Wells, "I've been thinking it over, Wells. You saved my life at the risk of your own. There's no doubt you're a changed man. Let Blake take you to the cavalry unit right now. You and your family can ride back north with them and go on back to Buffalo—you can take that job at the blacksmith shop. No one knows I was bringing you in. Get out of here and have a happy life."

Betty studied her husband's face in the fading light as he grinned and said, "Marshal, I appreciate your offer, but

I don't want to live the rest of my life looking over my shoulder. I'll face the law and take the consequences. I'll serve whatever time the judge gives me, and when I get out, I'll truly be a free man."

Wells's decision was hard for his wife to accept, but she knew it was the right thing to do. Claxton nodded, saying he understood.

The streets of Rawlins were well lighted as the stagecoach pulled in and came to a halt in front of the Buffalo Stage Line office. As the passengers were alighting, people began to gather around, asking if there had been Indian trouble. Molly, still crying, clung to Larry, and he embraced her before stepping out and offering her his hand. Then someone in the crowd recognized him, and there was an instant buzz among the townspeople, echoing his name.

A middle-aged man stepped up and said, "Good to see you, Larry. We all know why you're here. Vic Spain is over at the Loaded Dice Saloon. He said just this afternoon, right here in the street, that if you weren't on this stage, you were yellow."

Without comment, Larry leaned over and untied the leather thong that held the holster to his thigh. Thumbing tears from her cheeks, Molly said, "What are you doing?"

Unbuckling his gun belt, he replied, "I'm going over to the saloon unarmed to tell Spain I'll meet him in the street at sunrise."

Molly's blue eyes clouded. Still holding to her faith, she prayed as she and the others watched Mangrum's lanky frame amble across the street to the Loaded Dice. As soon as Larry had pushed through the batwings, Ross Blake broke from the group and dashed to the entrance of the saloon. Peering over the swinging doors, he observed the scene inside.

An instant hush came over the saloon as Larry Mangrum weaved his way among the tables to where Vic Spain sat playing cards. When Spain turned around to see what had brought the sudden silence, his homely face twisted with a snide grin. Shoving his chair back, he stood up, noticing at the same time that Larry was unarmed. He shifted the smoking cigar from one side of his mouth to the other, looking the young cowboy up and down with contempt.

Larry drew up and, holding the gunfighter with steady eyes, said thinly, "Just wanted you to know I'm in town, Spain. I'll meet you in the street at sunup."

Spain gave him a tight smile. "It's a date."

Larry turned and headed for the door, but just as he reached the batwings, Spain's words cut the still air. "Hey, Mangrum!"

Larry paused without turning around.

"I'll say one thing for you," said Spain with a gravelly voice. "You ain't yellow."

Larry gave the gunfighter a glance over his shoulder and then elbowed his way outside. There was an immediate hubbub in the saloon.

Ross Blake had started back to the stagecoach before Larry emerged from the saloon. The only thing Larry saw when he stepped into the street was Molly running toward him. He opened his arms and folded her in them.

"What happened?" she asked, her voice shaking.

"Nothing. We're set for sunup tomorrow morning." Looking past her, he saw Molly's parents standing by the coach, waiting for her. She quickly explained that Marshal Claxton had been taken to a doctor, but before he had left he told Wells that he would not advise the town marshal of the situation until morning. Her father could spend the night with her mother and her at the hotel.

Larry looked down into Molly's eyes. "I don't want you coming to the gunfight," he said firmly.

"I won't," she answered, lips quivering. "I couldn't stand to watch it."

Not caring who was observing them, Larry Mangrum kissed the lovely blonde tenderly, knowing it would be the last time. Hardly able to speak, he choked, "I'm going to see my parents now. I love you, Molly. I love you more than I could ever tell you. Please say good-bye to your parents and Mr. Blake for me." With that he released her, pivoted, and started to walk away.

"It isn't good-bye, Larry!" Molly said, breaking into sobs. "It just can't be! Something will happen. . . ."

Looking back through a wall of tears as he walked, the young man gave a slight wave of his hand and then turned and disappeared between two buildings.

That night at the hotel, Pete and Betty Wells were attempting to console their daughter as she lay across her bed, weeping. Suddenly there was a knock at the door. Betty stayed with Molly, speaking in soothing tones as Wells went to the door and pulled it open. Ross Blake stood there, his face was drawn and gray. In his hand was a sealed envelope.

"Come in, Ross," Wells said, swinging the door wider.

"I don't have time," Blake responded quietly. Extending the envelope toward Wells, he said, "I would appreciate it if you'd give this envelope to Larry Mangrum for me."

Wells took the envelope, looking puzzled. "I'll be glad to," he said. "But why don't you take it to him yourself?"

"You'll understand shortly," answered Blake in an even tone. "Just see that he gets it, okay?"

Wells nodded.

Blake gave him a strained smile and thanked him before wheeling and walking away. As if on a military mission, the former cavalry officer left the hotel and headed for the Loaded Dice Saloon.

Ross Blake knew he could never murder a man. Not even a man like Vic Spain. Blake would have to give the gunslinger a chance. Not an even chance, but a fair chance.

If he gave him an even one, Spain would outdraw him and kill him . . . and live to kill Larry Mangrum in the morning.

He stepped up on the porch of the saloon and looked over the batwings. He was glad to see that Spain was still at the same table, playing cards. Taking a deep breath, he loosened the revolver in his holster and shouldered through the swinging doors.

Chapter Thirteen

As soon as Ross Blake had left the hotel room, heading for the Loaded Dice Saloon, Pete Wells turned toward his wife and daughter.

"What do you think this is about?" his wife asked, staring at the envelope in his hand.

"I don't know," Pete replied, holding the envelope closer to his face, as if trying to read through it. "But I didn't like the look in his eyes."

"What do you mean?" she asked, standing up from the bed.

"I mean I'm going to do something I probably shouldn't." So saying, he tore open the envelope and pulled out the slip of paper, which he read aloud:

Dear Larry,

I couldn't let you go through with it. You have too much to live for. Don't feel sorry for me—I've made peace with myself, and now I can rest in peace, especially knowing that Vic Spain won't be around to bother you or anyone else. You marry that beautiful girl and have a happy life.

I sent a letter to Bill Owens at Buffalo, turning the

company over to him. He's to give you a job if you want it. No regrets, okay?

Your friend,
Ross Blake

Suddenly Molly sat up on the bed. "My God!" she blurted out, wiping the tears on her cheek. "He's going to shoot Vic Spain!"

Pete Wells had already snatched up his hat and was pulling open the door. "Get Larry!" he called over his shoulder. "I'm going to the Loaded Dice Saloon!"

Ross Blake could feel his temples pounding as he threaded his way among the tables through the smoky room. He had gone into many a battle knowing that he might face death, but never had he been so certain that he had seen his last sunrise.

Spain was at the table with two other men, seated at his right and left, with no one sitting in front of him. True to his custom, Spain was wearing a gun on each hip. Ross Blake circled around so as to face Spain head-on. Wiping his sweaty palms on his pants, he stepped to within three feet of the table.

Spain was laughing at a remark made by one of his friends, and Blake waited until the gunman looked up and saw him. To get the edge he needed, Blake started for his gun at the same time he called out, "Spain, I'm gonna kill you!"

Dropping the cards in his hand, Spain went for his right-hand gun while standing and shoving back the chair. His draw was like lightning, and despite the disadvantage of being seated, his revolver was in his hand before Blake's had even cleared leather. Spain's grin widened as he pulled the trigger and the hammer fell. But there was no accompanying roar; either the chamber was empty or the gun had misfired.

The gunfighter was already yanking out his left-hand

gun as Ross Blake's weapon went off with a roar, the slug drilling Spain dead center in the heart. Spain staggered, trying to rise to his feet, as blood spurted from the hole in his chest. Suddenly both his guns went off, the left one shooting into the floor planks and the right one catching Blake in the side, knocking him off his feet. Blake reeled backward, overturning one of the tables. When he hit the floor, he rolled himself over and blinked as he tried to focus on Spain, who lay sprawled a dozen feet from him.

Spain was not moving. There were vague forms shuffling around him. The bitter smell of gun smoke filled the air.

Someone knelt beside Blake and called his name, and he looked up to see Pete Wells staring down at him. Swallowing hard, he gasped, "Is he . . . is he dead?"

Wells nodded. "Just lie still. Someone's already gone for the doctor." He opened up Blake's shirt and examined the wound, then pronounced, "It's a good thing I didn't give that letter of yours to Larry Mangrum. I'm afraid you're going to live." His face broke out in a smile. "The bullet only creased your side. It looks like you're going to have to deliver it yourself."

Ross Blake found himself grinning, as well. He was glad to be alive, he realized. Though he knew that he would never forget or fully get over the death of his beloved Jenny, the events of the past few days had taught him the value of his own life.

Pete Wells tore off a length of Blake's shirt and wadded it up for Blake to hold over the wound. Just then Molly Wells and Larry Mangrum came rushing into the saloon and over to where Blake was lying.

"He's going to be all right," Pete Wells said, standing and taking his daughter in his arms as Larry stooped down beside Ross Blake. "I saw it all. Ross, here, plain outdrew him."

"That's a lie," Blake said, lifting himself up onto one elbow. "He had his gun out before I even got my hand around mine. But then the damnedest thing happened.

Spain had his gun out, ready to shoot me, but when he pulled the trigger, nothing happened. His gun misfired. It's lucky I'm alive."

"It wasn't luck," Molly declared, her eyes misting with tears. "It was God answering my prayers."

"But your prayers were for Larry," Blake reminded her.

Molly kneeled down and took one of Blake's hands in her own, while Larry put his arm around her shoulder. "Yes," she agreed. "But you don't think the good Lord would demand your life as the price for saving Larry's, do you? That would be an awfully harsh payment, indeed."

"Yes," Larry agreed. "Because then I wouldn't have had the chance to thank you for what you've done."

Blake looked up and saw the way that Larry and Molly were looking at each other. "Seeing you two together is all the thanks I'll ever need," he whispered. Suddenly he smiled and added, "Well, son, aren't you going to kiss her?"

Larry began to grin sheepishly. He glanced up at Molly's father and saw that he was nodding his approval. Larry's smile broadened, and everyone began to cheer as he pulled Molly to him and kissed her soundly on the lips.

Three days later Pete Wells stood trial and was convicted by the jury. Betty and Molly sat in the courtroom, their nerves tense. Larry was there with his parents, and Ross Blake sat next to them. Also in the courtroom, in a wheelchair with his arm in a sling, was U.S. Marshal John Claxton, his face a pasty white. The town's doctor was attending him.

Judge David W. Saylors, a heavyset bald-headed man in his sixties, heard the jury's verdict. Looking at Pete Wells, who sat at a nearby table, he said, "Will the accused please approach the bench for sentencing?"

Wells obeyed, placing himself before the judge.

"Do you have anything to say before I pronounce your sentence, Mr. Wells?"

Before Pete Wells could get a word out, John Claxton spoke up from his wheelchair. "Your Honor, as the arresting officer in this case, I would like to address the court, if I may."

Saylors nodded. "You may."

The doctor wheeled Claxton to the bench. The marshal spoke in a loud voice so everyone in the courtroom could hear him. He told of the change in Pete Wells . . . how he had been a responsible citizen in Buffalo for the past two years, and how he had saved the marshal's life at the risk of his own in the battle with the Sioux.

When Claxton had finished, the judge looked at Wells over his half-moon glasses and spoke sternly to him about his past as an outlaw. "The law must have its just due, Mr. Wells," he concluded sternly. "You are aware of that."

Wells nodded silently.

"Do you have anything to say in your defense before I pronounce sentence?"

"No, sir. The jury has rightly found me guilty. I must take what is coming to me."

"I sentence you to thirty years hard labor in the Wyoming Territorial Prison," Saylors said tonelessly.

Wells and his family were stunned. As a shocked silence ran through the courtroom, the judge's mouth split into a smile. "However," he continued, "in view of what I have just heard from the United States marshal, I am going to suspend your sentence, Mr. Wells. Instead you will be on probation, and I am assigning you to the custody of one of Wyoming's trusted citizens. Her name is Betty Wells. She will have to turn in a written annual report on your behavior for the next thirty years." Turning to Betty he asked, "Are you in agreement, Mrs. Wells?"

Dabbing at her eyes with a handkerchief, Betty said, "Yes! Oh, yes, Your Honor! Thank you!"

The gavel came down on the desk, and Saylors pronounced the court adjourned. Then with a broad smile, he said, "Mr. Wells, you are free to go."

Molly and Betty dashed over to Wells, embracing him. Then Molly left her parents and walked back to Larry. As the courtroom cleared, the curly-headed cowboy took Molly by the hand and led her to where his parents were standing.

With his face beaming, Larry said, "Dad, would you perform a wedding for a new employee of the Buffalo Stage Line and the woman he loves more than anything else in the world?"

FIFTH ANNIVERSARY
SPECIAL EDITION

STAGECOACH

Stagecoach 35:

BONANZA CITY
by Hank Mitchum

When bounty-hunter Rory Darson captures notorious outlaw Sonora Pike and boards a stagecoach bound for Bonanza City, Colorado, he does not know that Pike's sister, Natalie—whom Pike does not recognize—is aboard. With her is her shyster partner, out to swindle money from a wealthy mineowner.

Natalie, who fancies herself a witch, resolves to free her brother. In Bonanza City, she drugs the sheriff, stabs him, and releases Pike, who escapes. The sheriff lives but is unable to pursue Pike, and the job falls to Rory, who recaptures Pike and wins the approval of the townspeople—and of Hannah Campbell, the sheriff's beautiful daughter.

Meanwhile, Natalie and her partner, posing as cousins, are successfully luring the mineowner into their web. Natalie's seductive charms have mesmerized the mineowner, but then she becomes distracted by her growing rage against Rory Darson for imprisoning her brother again. As the rage turns to demonic obsession, her actions become more and more irrational, until at last she risks many lives to avenge the bounty hunter—including her own. But Rory Darson has found something to live for now, and he won't be defeated.

Read BONANZA CITY, on sale May 1988 wherever Bantam paperbacks are sold.